Brother Whale

Brother Whale

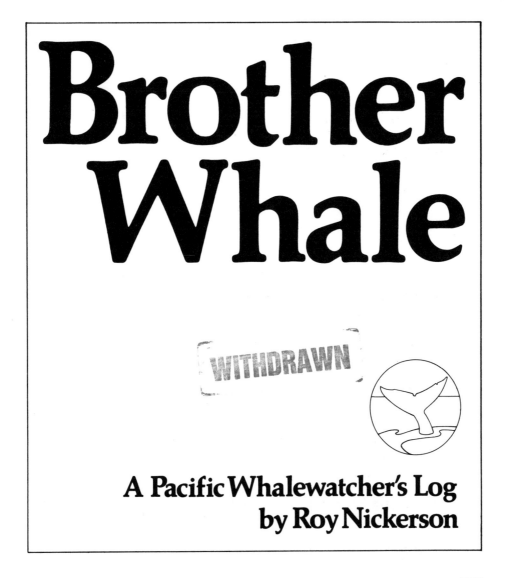

 WITHDRAWN

A Pacific Whalewatcher's Log
by Roy Nickerson

Chronicle Books / San Francisco

All photographs by the author.
Art on pages 40, 46-47, 52, 55, 60-61 and 62
by Larry Foster, General Whale.

Library of Congress Cataloging in Publication Data

Nickerson, Roy.
    Brother Whale.

     1. Whales—Pacific Ocean.   I. Title.
QL737.C4N47   599'.5   76-30828
ISBN 0-87701-087-0

Chronicle Books
870 Market Street
San Francisco, Ca. 94102

Contents

To Michael Schoepp
who is fifteen as this book goes to press,
who has watched the great whales with me,
and whose generation now inherits the responsibility
of making the world safe for the cetaceans

Foreword

In recent years there has been a tremendous increase in interest and awareness of the cetacean world. In the 1950s the United States was still actively hunting whales for meat and oil, and dolphins were kept in captivity only at Marineland of Florida, Miami Seaquarium, and Marineland of the Pacific.

With the 1960s came Flipper, the dolphin of television fame, Sea Life Park, Sea World, Marine World, many small parks with dolphins, and at last, an end to American whaling.

The early 1970s saw a continued expansion of marine parks, and in 1972, the Marine Mammal Protection Act gave all marine mammals under the United States jurisdiction nearly complete protection. Credit for this legislation should be given not only to our congressmen, but also to those who make the public aware of the uniqueness of whales and dolphins and the problems they face. The scientists who study them, the marine parks that enable the public to learn about them, and the authors who write about them are the ones responsible.

The future of all marine mammals is to a great degree in the hands of these people. Perhaps the 1970s will see the end of the slaughter of dolphins in tuna fishermen's nets, and if we are lucky, the end of international whaling. If so the credit should go to authors like Nickerson, Norris, and McIntyre, marine parks such as Sea Life Park, Sea World, and Marineland, the scientists studying the problems, and most importantly those people who listened and then did something.

Edward W. Shallenberger, Ph.D.
Vice President and Director of
Park Operations
Sea Life Park, Hawaii

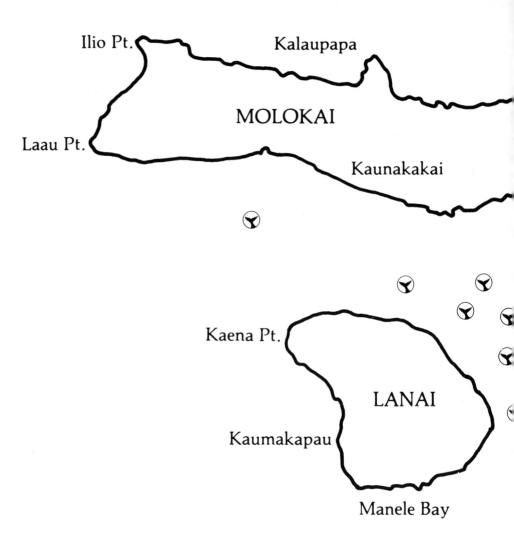

Humpback Whale Area

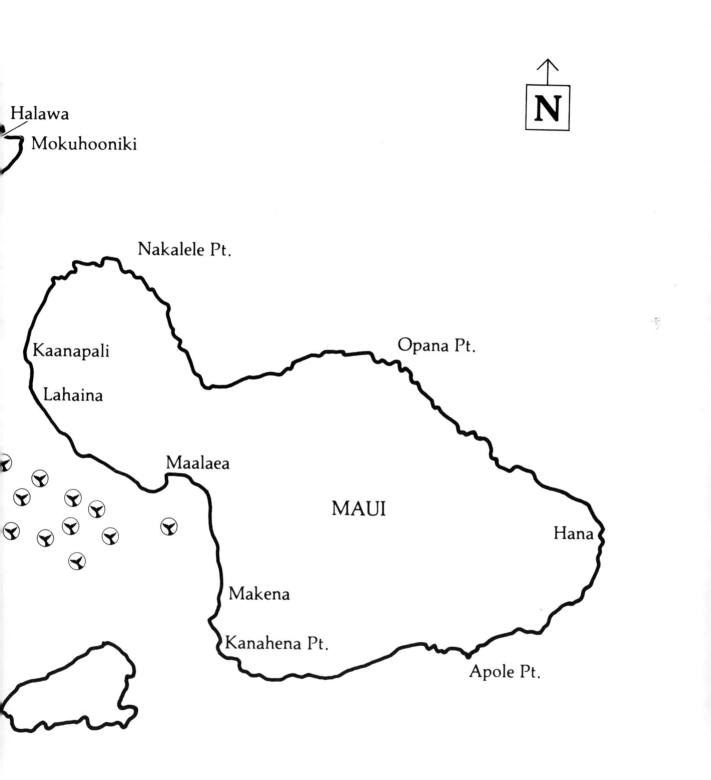

Halawa

Mokuhooniki

N

Nakalele Pt.

Opana Pt.

Kaanapali

Lahaina

Maalaea

MAUI

Hana

Makena

Kanahena Pt.

Apole Pt.

Introduction

This modest effort is not intended to pass as a definitive textbook. Rather, it is meant as an informal introduction to the wonderful world of the whales, both great and small, for those who have not previously studied the subject.

As an introduction, this book is meant to arouse interest and inspire readers to delve deeper into the subject. It is especially my hope that many people will read the book, look at the photographs, and then seek to learn still more about the cetaceans. Perhaps if they build a solid base of knowledge, they will then go out and tell the world that there is room enough on our planet for both human and cetacean; that the human race's cruel war against the cetaceans is an unnecessary one which must be stopped before it is too late. There are those who feel it is even now too late.

This book is directed primarily toward readers who live in the Pacific regions, for, particularly in the sections on whalewatching, it concentrates on the humpback whales who come to Hawaii and on the California gray whale, familiar to many who live along the Pacific Coast from California to Alaska. As an introduction to whales and dolphins in general, however, the book is valid anywhere. It is an introduction to all the whales, and it hopefully shows that just as there is a human family, so is there a family of cetaceans. It would be mutually beneficial if the one got to know the other.

Progress in halting the slaughter of the whales has been slow, a fact to which these pages often attest. And what sounds like encouraging news in this area is often awful news in disguise. For example, the Japanese have announced that they must consolidate their whale-hunting operations into one single company. They are doing so, however, not out of respect for the kill limitations forced upon them, but because there are fewer whales left for them to kill. And the Russians have just announced that they will cease all whaling in 1978, but this announcement, too, must be met with skepticism. Is it true or just more propaganda? If the announcement is true, was the decision made for the same reason that the Japanese have consolidated their whaling industry? These two nations account for 80 percent of the world's whale kill, but neither announcement is necessarily good news. The sad fact is, the whales may disappear before their friends succeed in protecting them.

The bibliography at the end of this book is intended not only to credit my major sources, but also to serve as a guide for those who would head for the library to learn more about the cetaceans.

Roy Nickerson
Lahaina, Maui

1

Beginnings

The great skeleton hung from the vaulted ceiling like a creature of someone's imagination. From its appearance, I could not imagine how large it had been in life. I couldn't even imagine anything that size having life. And yet, there it was, clearly labeled as the bones of a contemporary mammal . . . a whale.

This was a long time ago, back in the waning months of World War II, an event which had snatched me from high school while the ink on my diploma was still wet. I had never before been out of the primeval vastness of Nova Scotia and Maine. I had, however, been reared on tales of seafaring ancestors who roamed the world in a variety of pursuits; and I had been introduced early to the world of books. Through these circumstances, my first visit to New York City became a pilgrimage to the American Museum of Natural History, repository of the good works of my early heroes—the likes of photographers Martin and Osa Johnson, and naturalists Carl Akeley, and Roy Chapman Andrews. I had expected to find there in Central Park West the wonders of the veldt and jungles of Africa. These wonders were indeed there. But my attention had been snagged by something else—there was something magical about those bones.

I kept going back to the whale. I learned that this beast, which even now lives amongst us, is often more than twice as large as the largest of the extinct dinosaurs. And I knew that dinosaurs, representations of which had previously awed me, came to an ignoble end. They were merely cold-blooded reptiles which grew so large and became so slow that their stubby legs could not carry them quickly enough, and hunters wiped them from the earth.

The whales started out in the sea, as did all earth's creatures. Next they became amphibious, and then they became land-bound. Finally, perhaps they realized a truth that human beings, who are just beginning to talk of

aquaculture and cities under the ocean, have comprehended only fleetingly. For the ancient cetaceans headed once again to the sea, and there
they remained.

The whale is warmblooded, like you and me. Because it lives in the
world's oceans it can grow to such a giant size. What used to be legs and
feet when our whales' ancestors were land animals have evolved into
flippers and tailflukes. These appendages propel the huge bodies through
liquid space with both the ease and the beauty of birds flying through air.
The skeleton I saw that day showed that although the exterior covering
of a whale's flippers has fused over, underneath that covering—in the
skeleton—the "hand" and "finger" bones are still separate and distinct.
Also, because they live in water, and especially bouyant salt water,
gravity does not pull the whales' great bodies down; they don't have to
rely on legs and feet to support their bodies and move them around. The
whales may therefore grow to their immense size in the freedom of their
water world.

I became lost in those vast museum halls. I was so enthralled I paid no
attention to my direction. I realized that it was time to go, but I found an
exit only after I had inadvertently wandered once again along the bal-
cony which was not quite at eye level with the great whale remains. For a
moment, it occurred to me that it was rather indecent to display those
bones so unashamedly. I did not, however, have this feeling about the
bones of the giant prehistoric reptiles, nor the gorillas so masterfully
mounted by Akeley as if they were frozen there in life.

I stared for a moment, and then saw my exit. Mentally I said, "I'll be
seeing you, Brother Whale."

More than thirty years later I was aboard a boat which was mean-
dering slowly away from the port town of Lahaina on the Hawaiian island of Maui, peacefully in search of whales. This pleasant
day was like many I would experience, for I had by then made my home
in Lahaina, and I live there still. Somewhere in my family history was a
whaling captain, and sometimes I wonder if he had ever come to Lahaina. The city was once known as the whaling capital of the Pacific, not
because whales were hunted here, but because Lahaina was a convenient

Lahaina, historically a port for whalers working the Pacific hunting grounds.

center in the Pacific hunting grounds, and the whalers came here to provision their ships after sailing the open ocean for many months. They came here to partake of all the pleasures a port had to offer a sailor.

Sometimes during the 1820s to 1870s, the height of the old-time whaling industry, more than two hundred whalers would be anchored in the roadstead. Now I cruised on this very roadstead as often as I could from late November until the first of May, because during those months, these waters are the winter home of the great humpback whales. From the cold Arctic waters, where they romp and feed for half the year or more, they head south for Hawaii, and especially the waters off the western coast of Maui. They come here to mate; the next year they return to give birth after a gestation period of about eleven months. And the next year the juvenile returns to the waters of his birth with his family pod; some cetologists feel this is his only year of freedom before he becomes a parent himself, but this is one of the many secrets which the whales have not yet completely revealed.

The cycle in the humpbacks' life appears to be mate one year, give birth the next, and rest the third year; but again, this is guesswork not completely supported by research. Some cetologists also believe that the humpbacks practise monogamy, but only during a particular mating season. It appears that these whales live thirty years or more. That is, provided they make it through the increasingly scientific gauntlet laid down by modern whalers which the whales must run twice a year between their summer and winter homes!

When I first started whalewatching in Hawaii, in 1972, it was aboard an unlikely vessel named the *Coral See*, a 65-foot fiberglass tourist boat with viewing ports belowdecks left clear—"glass bottom," the advertisements say. Ordinarily, the *Coral See* takes tourists out to look at the coral in the reef which runs parallel to the shore off Lahaina. The boat's salty old skipper, Captain Les West, however, knows the ways of the sea well, and he knows how to handle the boat in his sleep. He also knows that one can coral-gaze almost any day of the week, so when the whales venture close enough to shore to be viewed from the *Coral See* he doesn't hesitate to head out for a look. Captain

The humpbacks' blows as seen from the Coral See. *Four whales can be seen here.*

West acknowledges that something of a mystical relationship exists between human beings and whales, and he knows without asking his passengers what their answer would be, should they have to choose between coral and cetacean.

And so, as December wears into January, Captain West always scans the waters even before leaving port. And if he sees blows or the telltale flashing gleam of light off a tremendous black back, he knows where to head. It was the Captain who really introduced me to the whales. Once settled in Lahaina I would go out once, twice, even three times a week in the hopes of catching a clear sustained view. For a while I had no luck at all. On days when I couldn't go out, I would listen to the stories Captain West told at the Lahaina Yacht Club after working hours: "You should have been with us today!" he would taunt. "You wouldn't believe it!"

Finally, one day it happened. The passengers were restricted to the main decks, but I was allowed to go topside, where two or three people familiar with boats could find a safe place to hang on and enjoy an unrestricted view. Captain West had spotted the blows. Out we went, a mile, a mile and a half, nearly two miles offshore; this was three times the usual cruise distance. The passengers anticipated something out of the ordinary, and the Captain finally announced that he hoped to provide them with some whalewatching. It was as if an electric charge had shot through the entire passenger load. None grumbled about missing the coral. All turned to scan the sea in the direction in which we were heading. For a while, nothing could be seen. Then, one by one, the humpbacks' blows appeared; there were four in all. Visually, the blows could be compared to the effect of puncturing a series of holes in a long steam pipe, invisible under the water. In quick succession, a number of tremendous vapor clouds shot upwards. Soon afterwards we could see the slight boiling of water as a black body broke the surface. One by one, each of the other three whales in the small pod followed suit.

As we approached, the Captain pointed the *Coral See* alongside the pod of whales rather than straight at them. He was obviously hoping to join the pod for a romp. The whales had disappeared, but not for long. One by one they broke surface, exposing first the spout, then the back. We were close enough now to see the somewhat triangular lump near each whale's head, behind which are located the twin blow holes. This lump is a sort of protective device, like a prow, which divides the water and

This show of flukes means that the whale will stay down for several minutes.

forces it to either side of the blow holes, rather than in them, as the whale swims forward. As the whales continued to arch to the surface, each long, unbelievably long, back was exposed—sometimes twenty-five to thirty feet from blow hole to fin; then another ten or fifteen feet to the massive flukes of the tail which can measure more than fifteen feet across.

I was to learn that the pattern of surfacing was always the same: first the head and blow hole would emerge and then submerge; the back would then be exposed, and as it submerged, the fin would flash on the surface. In deep dives, as the fin disappeared the flukes would come up. This perfectly circular motion makes it obvious how the whale got its name. The Anglo-Saxon forebears of *whale* are linked to the Norwegian *hwal* and the Dutch, *wal*; and all three mean wheel.

The marvelous, graceful wheeling motion continued, except now the flukes did not emerge. Later, after observing them for long periods of time, I was to learn to read the timetable involved: When a whale shows his flukes, he is sounding and will stay down for several minutes. But when he goes under without the flukes completing the wheel, he has made only a shallow dive and could reappear within seconds.

I heard the *Coral See*'s engines go into idle; Captain West knew what was coming. Because the whales and the boat were traveling in the same direction, the whales did not feel as though they were being attacked. They therefore felt at ease, and merely romped alongside us at our speed. But when we went into idle and advanced only by the boat's momentum, which quickly died, we became just another large hulk floating in the ocean. At that point the whales seemed to feel not only at ease, but curious as well. This was somewhat unusual; often the whales are startled by the sudden silence when the engine goes off.

We bobbed around for a moment or two, though it seemed much longer, without seeing anything. Then I heard the sound I will never forget, the sound that means a whale has surfaced right near by. It sounds like an explosion of steam, a sudden rush of unbelievable power, bursting from those giant tanks which are the whale's lungs, through a very narrow pipe, and out into unrestricted open space. This wonderful exploding hiss is followed almost instantly by the sound of the rush of water. When you aren't expecting it the sound combination is frightening; once familiar, it is thrilling.

A view from behind the twin blow holes.
The rows of bumps above the mouth are just visible.

And I heard these wondrous sounds once, twice, three times, four times. The whales were all around us, within twenty and thirty feet of the boat. They were not sounding; nor were they swimming away from us. They were slowly swimming *around* us. I looked right down the twin blow holes. I looked right down on those great and noble heads and saw what had only been described to me before: the rows of bumps both above and below the mouth and, in perfect geometry, across the top of the head. These bumps are referred to by cetologists as sensory knobs, and in the center of each is a single hair. The knobs and hair are believed to be tactile in nature—sensitive to the touch. The humpback can sense even the water currents he is passing through by means of these "warts," which are distinctive to the point of being ugly, as far as human notions of beauty are concerned.

For fully ten minutes the pod of four whales circled the *Coral See,* rushing by us from either direction, sometimes right at us, then veering off. Once one rushed us and then dived under our shallow-draft hull. There was a sudden bump; the whole boat jerked, but only slightly. A couple of women screamed, but more out of excitement than fear. (Back at port, a couple of hours later, a crewman swam under the hull and said he saw a short bare stretch where the algae had been scraped off the hull, but no damage had been done at all.)

The whales made one more slow pass at us. One appeared to stop momentarily while I aimed my camera at him. "Hello, again, Brother Whale," I said only slightly aloud.

"Huh?" asked the crewman who had joined me on the roof.

Captain West saw that the beautiful creatures had had their fill and were moving off. He engaged the engines again and headed for the coral gardens.

I n light of the fact that whales have been hunted, drawn, quartered, minced, and boiled for fully one thousand years, it is amazing how little is known about them. Our knowledge of the whale might be likened to the knowledge a blind person has of the cow, even though he has eaten beef daily.

Did I say one thousand years? The race to which we belong, the one we like to call human, has actually been hunting the whales and dolphins for far longer than that. It isn't really pertinent to lament this fact in view of man's even more savage behavior toward his own kind during all that time. But we well might ask the question, Why the whale, who has done nothing to cultivate animosity?

Some neolithic Norwegian cave drawings, dating from about 2200 B.C., clearly depict the hunting of porpoises. Records show that the Cretans hunted the porpoise in 3000 B.C. Phoenicians hunted sperm and right whales from 1000 B.C. to Roman times. The Mycenean Greeks showed an understanding that makes them shine out during that era: To them the dolphins, porpoises, and whales were sacred, and they did not hunt them at all.

Whaling as we know it started in the twelfth century A.D. in a land which, during the time I lived there I found otherwise to be lovelier than most—the Basque Country. This region consists of four provinces of southern France and four provinces of northern Spain at the border of those two countries. The Basque Country is so much a reality to the hardy souls who live there that they say there are only seven Basque provinces, instead of the eight which four and four usually equal. This is because the Navarre region transverses the border between France and Spain, and to the Basques of both countries it is one province.

It took just such an independent people to dare to attack a "fish" which was three times the length of their boats, and which weighed in excess of fifty and sixty tons. These first Basque whalers lived along the Bay of Biscay, which experienced seasonal whale traffic. They maintained regular watches on stone towers at high points near the shore's edge. When the tower watch sighted spouts out in the bay, they lit fires to send up signals of smoke. Quickly the hunters would appear and put out in rowboats. Once the whale died its slow death at the hand of many harpooners, he was hauled up on the beach, and there the oil was rendered in great open pots. Whatever one's sentiments are about whaling, it's impossible not to admire the daring of these early Basques setting off in their flimsy boats to combat the great leviathan.

At first the early whalers went after what were called "floaters," whales which floated on the water's surface even in death. One kind of whale was called the right whale, and it is still known as that; it was "right" because it was the first of the floaters that they harvested out at sea. Another early target was the bowhead whale; later, the sperm whale was sought.

The dorsal fin, which distinguishes the humpback as a rorqual.

Human history does indeed repeat itself, yet we seem never to learn from experience. Down through the centuries, a pattern has developed in whaling: Whalers kill off one kind of whale to the verge of extinction in one vicinity, and are thus forced to muster greater daring and to go farther afield to find the same whale. Then, because of diminishing numbers, the hunters start attacking other kinds of whales, kinds which weren't originally considered "right." Eventually the "floaters" became so scarce that whalers went after the "sinkers," and they had to develop more sophisticated means of fishing to do so. Generally, the "sinkers"—which had the annoying ability to swim faster than other whales, and were thus more difficult to catch—are the rorquals, the whales with a dorsal fin. These included the blue whale, the fin, the sei, the Bryde's, and the minke. In a genus to itself is the humpback, also a rorqual, though some cetologists put it in a family by itself, rather than classify it as such. (The humpback is family Megaptera; the others, Balaenoptera.)

Killing the humpback! When I first read that, I felt somewhat the same as when I was very young, and for the first time I was made to understand that in wars they used *real* bullets—that war was not just a game like the one I played in my backyard with the other kids, where after being "killed" we got up and went home to dinner. And then only recently I was researching in a book called *Lost Leviathan*, by F. D. Ommanney. In it were snapshots the author had taken from the bridge of a modern whaling vessel in the waters of New Zealand, where the humpback is still hunted. Looking down the backs of a pod of humpbacks which was fleeing the hunter boat, a view which had come to be so familiar to me during my whalewatching cruises off Maui, well . . . there was something unbelievable about those photos. I just couldn't accept the fact that someone was actually running down my humpbacks to kill them. Without attempting to create literary dramatics, I honestly felt as though Dr. Ommanney had stumbled onto and photographed a murder.

The intrepid Basques found that the whales soon learned not to come too close to shore, so they took to the sea in what were, by today's standards, frighteningly small boats. They stayed out for days, then weeks, and eventually months, in pursuit of the whale. They went north to Spitsbergen, then west across the Atlantic to the seas off Newfoundland. The Basques fished, whaled, and without a doubt sought supplies on land, on the North American continent, three centuries before Columbus sailed to the more distant climes of that same continent.

And the Basques became the master teachers in the whaling industry, which spread to the French, to the descendents of those prehistoric Norse who had recorded their dolphin hunts in cave paintings, to the Dutch, the English, and the Germans. The New England Yankees got into the act in about 1820, and soon afterward they came to Hawaii. The Norwegians dominated the field, except in the Yankee whaling grounds, until the mid-sixties. Today the primary whalers are the Japanese and the Russians. They have become the heavies of the international whaling cartel because of the volume they deal in. In my book, however, they are no more guilty than our good friends the Australians and New Zealanders. The harpoon does its work no matter what the nationality of the harpooner.

From the 1820s to the 1870s the New England whaler was king of the industry. At this time the Yankee was concentrating on sperm whaling because the right and bowhead stocks had been so reduced that they were hard to find. It is said that at the height of the Yankee fleet a total of 736 ships out of various New England towns all sailed the high seas in search of the whale. At the same time all the other nations of the world engaged in whaling had a total of some 200 ships assigned to the same task. The American whalers would stay out of port as long as five years at a time, until their holds and even, in some instances, their decks were filled to capacity with sperm oil, spermaceti, and whalebone. (Spermaceti is a waxy solid which separates from the whale oil, and is found especially concentrated in the "case," or head receptacle. Cetologists are studying the idea that this great well of "wax" in the head serves as a gatherer and conductor of sound for the sperm whale. According to the *Encyclopedia Brittanica*, between 1830 and 1840, American whalers brought in 41,241,310 gallons of sperm oil as well as great quantities of oil from baleen whales.) When they returned to port, as often as not the ordinary seaman would learn that all he had to show for five years at sea was five years of free room and board and lots of wasted sweat. The shipowners, of course, got the lion's share of the revenues from the sale of the whale parts. The captain was well paid; his mates, a little less so. The whale magnates had a formula which usually resulted in the ordinary deckhand receiving one two-hundredth of the cargo's value. While at sea, the sailor bought clothing and tobacco and borrowed cash advances for rare excursions ashore on credit against his share. The latter, it is recorded, often came out to exactly what he owed the "company store."

The Pacific fleet began to thin out by 1860, both because the whales were more difficult to find, and because the discovery of oil in Pennsylvania eliminated much of the American need, or demand, for whale oil. The fleet died forever in 1871 when, after sailing north from Hawaii, it was trapped in an ice floe near Point Barrow. The greedy whaling skippers wanted to remain until the last possible whale had been killed, and they gambled that they would know far enough in advance when to sail so as to outdistance the floe. It was a gamble they all lost, for the entire fleet was caught in a sudden freeze, crushed, and sent to the bottom.

A wholesaler of scrimshaw and ivory who lives on Lahaina, Robert B. Hartman, recently came into possession of an old scrapbook which is a treasure chest of whaling lore. It apparently came from a New England whaling family and consists of newspaper clippings which go back as far as 1895. Many of the clippings are of interviews made with the old men who, in their youth, had gone to sea in search of whales. The ancient salts talk of whaling days which are history to us; they even recall the days when the whalers came to Hawaii for a rest from their toils and to provision their ships. All the reference books in the world cannot convey what it was really like the way these personal interviews do.

And one thing about the scrapbook that is especially interesting: Even in those days, newspapers and the people they quoted expressed fears that the whales were being hunted to extinction. For example, a clipping from the *Boston Herald*, dated July 29, 1928, bears this head: "50-ton Whales Have Little Chance When Harpoon Gun Shoots." This was followed by the subhead, "So They're Fast Vanishing, with the Oil and Bones that Commerce Values." The story read in part as follows:

> . . . the 150-pound harpoon was lifted, with an arrow head-point sharp as an ice pick—containing five pounds of explosive ready to detonate four seconds after the great spear was fired. . . . At 50 yards the gun was pointed at the great bull [whale] and barked its

smothered "blam." The harpoon leaped straight for the whale and struck with a soft thud 10 feet back from the tip of the nose.

For a moment nothing happened. Then the whale threw his huge tail into the air, sank the forward half of his body into the sea and started to dive just as the muffled report came from the time-exploding charge. He rolled over and was dead.

Such is modern whaling. Sometimes, as along the North Pacific coast, airplanes are used to spot the whales and signal or fly back with the location for the fast motorships with their guns and time fuses. The whale consequently has been fast disappearing. While previously he had a chance to escape, he now has slight opportunity. Once the harpoon gun strikes him, it is all over.

The seafaring nations of the world are awakening to the fact that they cannot afford to lose the whale: he is too valuable . . .

The Carnegie Institution at Washington has been gathering data for a history of the whale. Dr. Remington Kellogg, research associate [there] . . . has found skeletons which appear to prove that the whale was once a great land animal that took to the water and stayed there because he likes it better. . . . Ancient whales changed their limbs into flippers. The fingers are still very much like hands with fingers. Some whales even have a thumb. . . .

T he Hartman scrapbook is full of the kinds of information that you can't find in textbooks or reference works. For instance, just as World War II gave the whale stocks a breathing spell in which to breed without interruption, a "war" of another sort may have saved them from the Yankee whaler during the Prohibition era! From the *Boston Herald* of May 29, 1925:

New York, May 28—Early on Tuesday morning, Capt. Gustav Wittstein of the North German Lloyd liner *Luetzow*, which arrived today at Hoboken, saw the largest school of whales that he has ever seen in his 33 years in the North Atlantic service. . . .

. . . there were hundreds of them. . . .

"The only way I can account for it is that probably the whalers have gone into the rum running business and for that reason are giving the whales a chance to live in peace."

Even in this century there were references to Hawaii, or the Sandwich Islands, as Captain Cook named them for the first lord of the admiralty, the Earl of Sandwich. For example, On October 29, 1929, *The Boston Traveler*, carried an article on a retired whaling captain named George Smith:

> The first three voyages of the captain's career occupied more than 15 years. Cargoes of oil were shipped home from New Zealand and from the Sandwich Islands.
> In these regions he pursued the finback, the humpback and the sperm whale. . . . Once the captain caught the disease known as the beri beri due to a lack of certain mineral salts in the diet and had to be shipped home.

(Serves the old blighter right!)

Of obvious personal interest to me, considering that the captain involved is my namesake, was an advertisement and handbill contained in the Hartman scrapbook. It read, "I Have Seen the Great Right Whale—Now at Otis Wharf. . . . She was captured or killed in Provincetown, Mass., Harbor, January 15, 1909, by Capt. Joshua Nickerson, an old retired whaler. . . ." The flyer said the bones from the whale were 34 feet, 9 inches in overall length.

In 1974, a remarkable California woman named Joan McIntyre assembled a variety of published and unpublished writings concerning current investigations into the whale as an intelligent, thinking—perhaps reasoning—animal. The anthology is called *Mind in* *the Water.* (The proceeds of the book sales go to Project Jonah, one of the first of the more sensible "save the whales" organizations.) Just a hint of the theme of this modern book was found in another Hartman scrapbook clipping, this one from the January 28, 1922, edition of the *Boston Transcript*: "Mr. Brown can tell of the habits of whales . . . and he thinks that they are human, temperamental and very intelligent. 'Why, I've been told by whalers who have watched them at play that they have their preferences, same as among folks. A bull whale will pat his mate, not very lightly maybe but in a manner that cannot be mistaken for anything but a caress. . . .'"

Mr. Brown was Frank E. Brown of New Bedford, Massachusetts, maker of whaling guns and lances all his life, whose job kept him in constant contact with a variety of whaling men and their skippers. Think of the number of different observations—and yarns—he heard! He obviously had much data to refer to before arriving at his own conclusions.

When the great whales' numbers began to thin out in the traditional hunting grounds of the North Pacific, North Atlantic, the Indian Ocean off the eastern coast of Africa, as well as other smaller seas, the whalers who had hunted off New Zealand and Australia surmised that there must be prey farther down toward the Antarctic. The Norwegians were the first to prove this hunch. This following quick summation of the results of that guess was given in a scrapbook clipping from the *New York Times Magazine* dated June 27, 1926:

> Whaling Still Yields Profits—Industry the New Englanders Abandoned Brings Huge Returns to Hardy Norwegians Who Follow the "Great Fish" in the Cold Antarctic
>
> . . . [D]ue to the discovery of new hunting grounds in the Antarctic . . . the produce of these grounds has far surpassed in amount and value that of the entire Yankee fleet even in the palmy days of the last century.
>
> The zenith of the New England whaling industry was in the quarter century between 1835 and 1860. In that period, with about 600 vessels engaged in the chase, the annual return averaged 150,000 barrels of oil. Recent records from the Antarctic show that

Captain Nickerson's handbill, from the Hartman scrapbook.

vessels licensed in the Falkland Islands and dependencies alone—
only a part of the vast whaling grounds around the South Pole—
have brought home some 600,000 barrels of oil a year. . . ."

The article stated that in the years 1835 to 1860, the average yearly value
of the bone and oil take was $8 million. In the mid-'20s when the article
was written—the average yearly value was $15 million.

Perhaps I am prejudiced because I have been a newspaper reporter
for much of my life, but it seems to me that these clippings—
reports made at the actual time when the events were occurring,
and interviews quoting the living words of those who had participated in
whaling events—add spontaneity and authenticity—in short, life—
which a historic rendering or retelling of facts lacks. This is why I'm
grateful to Bob Hartman for sharing this scrapbook with me.

Most of the clippings were carefully dated and the source was duly
noted. One which I liked in particular, however, had no such notation.
Comparing type, and judging from dates of clippings that come before
and after, I would think this gem came from the *Boston Transcript* sometime in 1928. It is an interview with Timothy Woodberry of Beverly Cove,
Massachusetts. He is identified as a whaler and a carpenter. The story is
prefaced by the notation that he sailed out of Boston on a four-year
whaling trip in 1865. His share of those four years' labors came to a mere
$380. "As a carpenter in recent years he has been making that much
money in 48 days," the interviewer commented. Then he started quoting
Whaler Woodberry:

We were 145 days making the voyage to Honolulu. You can do it
now in 20. Nothing ever looked better to me than that land about
Honolulu Harbor, as we sailed past Diamond Head. Climbing aloft
with my watch to furl sail, I looked shoreward and saw a hill beautiful with flowers, orange, lemon and lime trees, with a white
church and bamboo huts. So sweet a fragrance was wafted out over
the water that I thought it was the Garden of Eden.

A few days later we got away in the bark *Stephanie* after whales;

cruised over the Pacific grounds until May with fair luck, and then put into port near Yokohama, Japan, for wood and water. While lying here, one of our best boatsteerers stole $40 in gold from the captain's locker and swam ashore.

* * *

[On the return voyage] . . . we lay in the stream at Honolulu three weeks, getting out our oil and refitting. We had shore leave every evening and used to go up to the National Hotel, the only large building in town. All the others were bamboo huts, and were connected by paths, for there were no streets.

If you wanted to, you could hire a horse and ride out into the country. Horses were cheap. You could ride him until he dropped. All the owner asked was you bring in saddle and bridle.

Honolulu in those days was just a rambling town of 3,500; dull enough except when the fleet was in.

(Honolulu now has a population of about 350,000. In the 1970 census it ranked forty-fourth in size among American cities, only two behind Miami, which it resembles in the Waikiki area!)

T he last clipping I copied from the Hartman scrapbook was a letter to the editor of the *Boston Herald*, May 20, 1928. This letter could have been written today, and is another example of "Everyone talks about the weather, but no one does anything about it." The letter writer was one Nathan Haskell Dole of Boston.

No one who reads the daily newspapers can have failed to notice that the whale is all the time occupying more and more attention. . . .

The profits of this business are so enormous that, according to reports, there is a likelihood of the total extinction of all whales, and a movement has been set afoot to protect them, by international agreement, just as the seals on the Pribylof Islands have been salvaged. Think how much richer the world would have been if the last pair of dodos had been permitted to live and restock. . . .

A humpback, pectoral flippers flailing like arms, breaching to land on his back.

But these early glimmers of conservationist insight didn't have much effect, and the decline of the American whaling industry by no means meant the end of whaling in general. Only three years before the Pacific fleet went under, a Norwegian named Svend Foyn had invented the harpoon gun. Thus 1868 is known as the year when modern whaling was born. With Foyn's invention the death knell for whales as secure members of the world's population was sounded.

The harpoon gun made today's indiscriminate whaling possible. Although early forays against the whales obviously cut into their numbers, it is just possible that each species could have survived the old methods. The explosive harpoon, however, opened up a new kind of whaling which makes it a certainty that the world's whales will perish without effective protection.

In early whaling, a whole ship pitted all its resources against one whale at a time—first in the kill, and then in the slow backbreaking work of processing the carcass and storing the valuable products. One aspect of these methods makes it at least conceivable that even in the old days the whale populations could have been decimated to the point of no return. Charles M. Scammon, in his classic *Marine Mammals of the Pacific Northwestern Coast of North America*, and Frank M. Bullen, an ancient mariner who wrote of his years as a whaler in novel form in his wonderful *Cruise of the Cachalot*, both state that the old-time whalers had no compunctions against harpooning a days-old baby in order to take advantage of the mother's reluctance to abandon it, thus making herself an easy target. The whalers cared nothing for stock management, nor did they think about the future.

With Foyn's invention an explosive charge is shot into one whale after another in the same pod. Each carcass is flagged and the hunter ship moves on, wiping out an entire pod at a time. A factory ship then comes along and picks up the pieces, so to speak. The hunter goes on looking for further prey, unfettered by the need to process the whale it had just killed, as the old-time whalers had to do. In the early days, the whales died one at a time; today's "progressive" technology allows a whole family to be wiped out at once.

According to French whale authority Paul Budker, during the 1930-31 whaling season 38 factory ships and 184 catchers, or hunters, were working the Antarctic grounds. He also records that this was the first year in

which the price of whale oil dipped. This drop served to wake up the
whaling companies, warning them that their industry, too, could decline.
Until then, they had thought themselves beyond the variables which
affected the rest of the business world. Budker says that the price fluc-
tuation prompted whaling companies to understand that both their profits and the animals from which they derived their profits needed some
protection. This realization was the beginning of what was to become the
International Whaling Commission (IWC).

On September 24, 1931, twenty-six countries at the assembly of the
League of Nations in Geneva approved of the formation of an
International Convention for the Regulation of Whaling. The
representatives of these nations agreed upon a quota of whales to be
killed for the 1931–32 season.

The first actual IWC meeting was held in 1937, and was called the
London Conference. The whaling nations, all at least minimally concerned about the depleting whale stocks in the world's oceans, met that
first time under the motto, "Exploitation without destruction." As is
common today, economists and scientists battled it out, but the conference did manage to establish some kill quotas. Even during that fateful
wartime season of 1939–40, however, some whaling continued. A total of
twenty-eight factory ships went out then. After that, humans were pre-
occupied with killing each other off. The factory ships were turned into
tankers for the war effort, and the whales had a rest. The IWC was re-
affirmed in 1946, and the mental giants present at the conference that
year finally agreed that the whale quota could no longer be simply stated
as a certain number of whales. They realized that different species of
whales grow to be different sizes, and thus yield different amounts of oil.
Therefore, the commission came up with what is known as the BWU—
the blue whale unit. The blue whale is the largest of all the cetaceans; it
can reach one hundred feet in length. A formula was developed whereby
one blue whale equaled two finbacks, two and a half humpbacks, or six
sei whales. Quotas were then decided upon based on BWU values. This
system, if you look at it, was a mixed blessing. It did mean that the nearly
extinct blue whale could be killed two and a half times less frequently
than the humpback whale, for instance. But by the same token, it also

meant that the endangered humpback could be hunted two and a half times more freely than the nearly extinct blue.

That is, if someone was watching.

After all, like most international organizations, the IWC operated on the honor system. There may be honor among thieves, but there is none among nations. The overriding interest of any country is national interest. The main function of the IWC is the same as that of the United Nations, and the ruling principle is the same: voluntary cooperation of members. Anyone who believes that a whaling ship which is out of sight and out of touch with monitors or whalers of other nations will not take a prohibited species or an extra whale above their allotted count is naive indeed. I am reminded of the comment I read following the Gary Powers/ U-2 spying incident: "Everyone knows that every nation is spying on every other nation. What is shocking about this incident is, the Americans allowed themselves to get caught." And that is the highest crime that nations can commit against the IWC: not the breaking of international agreements, but getting caught at it.

Still, the BWU quotas were somewhat better than Britain's first attempt to control the whale kill. In *Lost Leviathan*, F. D. Ommanney writes that the British government first became concerned over the decreasing size of the whale stocks as far back as 1908, and by 1917 the government had established a per-barrel tax on whale oil. On the plus side of this move, the tax eventually funded the Discovery Program, which ended up in the Antarctic making a scientific study of whale physiology. Previously, whalers had hacked the animals up without really seeing what they were looking at, and very little was known by anyone about the great beasts.

Unfortunately, the whale-oil tax simultaneously encouraged the development of floating whaling factories away from land controlled by the British; oil processed on the open sea was not subject to the tax. Dr. Ommanney reports that in the end the tax drove kills up, not down. In the 1937–38 Antarctic season, for example, he says a total of some 55,000 whales were killed, as compared with 38,000 in 1929–30, and 43,000 in 1930–31, when there were no floating factories.

The IWC quotas went into effect under the United Nations in postwar years. Still, it is reported that in the 1950s, between 20,000 and 25,000 whales were killed each year. Meanwhile, in many of the IWC member nations the whaling industry declined and finally died. The American industry had effectively disappeared by the mid-1920s. The last British whaler was taken over by the Japanese in 1957. The Dutch stopped whaling in 1964, ending centuries of tradition. The last Norwegian ship went to the southern grounds in 1967. In 1971, the IWC decided to abandon the BWU in favor of separate species quotas, thus protecting the last remnants of some critically endangered species.

On the other hand, in the 1960s the Russians arrived in the Antarctic grounds with a fleet that included the 36,000-ton *Sovietskaya Ukraina*, the world's largest factory ship, thereby demonstrating that the development of whaling technology had by no means stopped. Shortly thereafter Japan reentered the whaling scene, and these two countries continue to be the largest whaling nations today. Together they account for 80 percent of the whales killed in the world. Thus, the slaughter continues.

Both the Russians, with their new ship, and the Japanese with consolidated fleets, demanded increased kill quotas in the 1970s. The 1975–76 season found the IWC permitting the death of 9,360 minke whales, 585 fins, 2,230 seis, 1,363 Brydes, and 19,040 sperm. A total of some 9,000 fewer whales was allowed for the 1976–77 season in all; again, it is sad to remark that the reduction is not because the whaling nations care about the fate of the whales, but because they know they cannot find more than that number of whales to kill.

Why do they go on? What is it that modern society needs from the bodies of whales? The Japanese claim that six percent of their country's protein comes from whale meat. Their need for this cheap meat source is questionable, as we shall see in Chapter 6.

A major export of Japan is pet food, but England, once an important customer, was civilized enough to stop importing Japanese pet food in 1975 because it was made from whale meat. However, other countries continue to feed their cats and dogs on whale. Fertilizer is made from the whale, and a prime customer for that product is our good neighbor to the south, Mexico, which otherwise has supported whale conservation efforts. Mexico apparently feels enough justification in the fact that the whales weren't killed by Mexican whalers.

Poultry feed and cattle fodder come from whales.

Lipstick, varnishes and stains, margarine, cold cream—these are all made from whale oil. And not only the space vehicles but the airplanes and submarines of some nations are lubricated with greases and oils made from the whale. Sarah Riedman and Elton Gustafson, in their book *Home Is the Sea: For Whales*, report that hormones for medical use are taken from the pituitary, pancreas, thyroid, and various other glands of the whale.

Is there any justification for whaling today? The answer is a resounding No. Not one need is being met in the whale harvest that cannot be met with less drastic effect some other way. The products we derive from whales are either dispensable or replaceable. The whales themselves are not.

Drawing by Larry Foster, General Whale

*Hundreds of thousands of stenellas are destroyed each year
by the American yellowfin tuna fisheries.*

Some Basic Cetology

One of the most comforting aspects of writing about whales is the fact that so little is really known about them, especially regarding the habits of the living animals. Only by collecting bits and pieces such as those gleaned from the Hartman scrapbook clippings, and from studying the few authoritative books on the subject can we start to fit together pieces of a gigantic puzzle which, in truth, may never come together completely. Most scientists, researchers, and amateur naturalists such as myself can safely write, "It is believed," or, "It appears," and fear only a contradiction based on theory, not on fact. That's one thing that made my several years of whalewatching cruises in the Lahaina Roadstead so fascinating: I was often able to confirm the "it appears" observations of others; and sometimes I was able to make first-time "it appears" observations of my own. Few fields remain so unexplored today.

But some basic tools of the trade do exist. Among the most useful, as with any specialized field, is the agreed-upon terminology. After all, some of the thrill of whalewatching is lost if you can't identify the animals you see. For example, when one first gets into the whalewatching business, the question usually arises, What's the difference between a dolphin, a porpoise, and a whale? A number of complicated scientific distinctions exist for those serious students who need them, but basically the main difference is size.

Captain W. F. J. Morzer Bruyns is an acknowledged international expert on the classification of whales. He is the author of *The Field Guide of Whales and Dolphins*, published in 1971 in Holland and now available in English. The Captain says that, generally speaking, a whale is a cetacean (that is, a member of the order Cetacea) which is more than thirty feet in length; a dolphin is a cetacean between six and thirty feet long; and a porpoise is any cetacean less than six feet long. This is a fair generality, but has its flaws. For instance, the beaked whales range from thirteen to thirty feet in length, the pygmy sperm whale averages nine feet, and the pygmy right whale averages thirteen feet. Yet these animals would never be classified as dolphins.

Dolphins and porpoises can be distinguished from whales according to other criterion besides length. To a certain extent, for example, it may be said that the head of a porpoise is blunter than that of the dolphin. This is true to the extent that the smaller dolphins have what is called a beak. However, when you get to the larger dolphins, such as the pilot whale and the orca, this distinction does not apply.

Custom plays a large part in cetacean nomenclature. Some names are just convenient handles rather than scientific descriptions. Here in Hawaii we see two of the little guys in particular, and they are both called dolphins when referred to specifically: the bottlenose dolphin and the spinner dolphin. Yet when they come up to a boat and start to clown around, someone invariably shouts, "Look at the porpoises!" and no one argues.

Still, a bit of cetological terminology is helpful in identifying these great sea mammals and distinguishing one species from another. The standard zoological classification system divides cetaceans into two groups, or suborders. The whales with baleen—a structure resembling a giant bony sieve or strainer attached to the upper jaw in place of teeth—are called Mysticeti. (This word comes from the Greek for mustache, *mysta*.) Whales with teeth are Odontoceti, a Latin word that anyone who has visited the dentist will be able to translate. Apparently the territory to which a particular type of whale adapted, and thus the food available to it, influenced which species evolved with teeth and which with baleen—that is, which evolved as Odontoceti, and which as Mysticeti.

Of the great whales—those which reach more than thirty feet in length at maturity—the best known is the sperm whale. The sperm whale is the largest toothed whale. It is generally drawn in cartoons with a smile and a spout of water coming out of the top of its head. Though the sperm whale is well known, because of its diet of cuttlefish and sea mollusks it stays out in the oceans, rarely coming within sight of land; it also tends to remain in warmer waters, rarely venturing beyond 40 degrees north or 40 south. (Most scrimshaw—the delicate etching of drawings on whale ivory—is done on sperm whale teeth.) The bottlenose whale, not to be confused with the popular bottlenose dolphin of "Flipper" fame, is also a

Spotted dolphins off Lanai

toothed whale. This whale is less accessible than the sperm whale and has fewer teeth. The beluga, a "whale" which averages fifteen feet in length, has some small teeth. Porpoises and dolphins all have teeth of varying amounts. The Odontoceti, both great and small, have a head structure much like other mammals—with the jaw at the bottom. In baleen whales, however, while the skeleton is much the same as Odontoceti species, the build-up of flesh in the lower head region makes the jaw appear to lie toward the top of the head.

Most species of great whales are Mysticeti, baleen whales, with the great strainers, the baleen, affixed in rows in the upper jaw where teeth would ordinarily be found. The baleen whale dives after its food, closes its mouth, and then forces the water out through the baleen with its great tongue, trapping the fish, which cannot pass through the baleen, inside its mouth.

A baleen whale is able to scoop up tremendous amounts of water as it surges after swarms of krill or zooplankton, the tiny animals that drift through the sea in huge passive floating colonies. The whale's enormous capacity is due to a remarkable characteristic of its skin. As the throat and stomach fill up, either with water which will soon be expelled or with food awaiting digestion, the skin stretches. Along the neck and belly area are lines of what look and act much like the folds in an accordion. These folds are called ventral (belly-side) grooves. Most baleen whales have them, and with the exception of the humpback and the California (or Pacific) gray whales, from seventy to a hundred of these pleats run from the chin to the navel area. The humpback has from fourteen to twenty grooves. On the humpback, the pleats are wider, and thus fewer are needed. The gray whale has only two to four grooves.

Whether a whale has teeth or baleen, it never chews its food. Both kinds of structures are used to hold the food, preventing it from escaping until it is advanced to the stomach. Many cetaceans have a multi-stomach system. The bottlenose dolphin, for instance, has three stomachs, the first of which is referred to as a crop. In the crop the bones of fish are segregated out and then regurgitated, while the fish's flesh goes on to the main stomach. (On land, three stomachs and sometimes four are found not only in certain ungulates such as the cow, distant and ancient relatives of the whale, but also in some monkeys.)

With these two larger categories, the toothed and baleen whales, accounted for, a few other terms associated with cetaceans will be helpful.

Dolphins and porpoises are Odontoceti, toothed cetaceans, as was mentioned. The Latin designation for dolphin is Delphininae; this classification refers to a subfamily which includes many species of dolphin. The "common" dolphin is *Delphinus delphis*. The subfamily Delphininae also includes many species of porpoise. The word porpoise itself comes to English by way of the French term *porc poisson*, pig fish, reference to the tendency of the porpoise's nose to be blunter than that of the dolphin.

Another term which you will come across often is *rorqual*. A rorqual is a member of the family of whales with a dorsal fin (a fin on the midback). There are two types, or genera, of rorquals: (1) the finback, which includes the blue, fin, sei, Bryde's, and minke whales, and (2) the humpback whale. All rorquals are baleen whales. The right, gray, and sperm whales do not have dorsal fins, and therefore are not classified as rorquals. The right and gray are baleen whales; the sperm, as noted earlier, is the largest of the toothed whales.

At this point it is generally customary to launch into a discussion of comparative size. The point need not be labored. The largest of the whales is the blue whale, which can grow to more than 100 feet in length. By comparison, the largest of the land creatures known to have existed was the brontosaurus, which grew to some 70 feet. At 150 tons, as various writers have pointed out, the blue whale equals 30 elephants, 100 cows, or 2,000 human beings.

The blue whale, however, is not the whale most people see. The most frequently sighted whales are the humpback and gray, reaching 45 and 50 feet at maturity. The sperm whale goes another 10 feet. From drawings and photographs, I had always thought the unique narwhal, with its unicorn-like tusk, grew to be very large. I discover, however, that the narwhal averages only 25 feet, including the tusk, which averages 6 to 8 feet in length. The killer whale, or orca, is less than 30 feet long, and thus is not really a whale but a dolphin. The orca is a good example of the need to take into consideration customary name use rather than relying solely on scientific terminology when trying to identify a cetacean in the wild.

At the risk of digressing, I hasten to come to the defense of the orca. He has a much-maligned reputation. Just as he is not a true whale, at least in the popular sense neither is the orca a brutal killer. He *is* a killer among his own whale–dolphin kind—he is the only cetacean to actively and habitually go looking for warmblooded prey, and his victims are often other cetaceans. But the popular belief that he is a mankiller is

Grey whale and calf.

Drawing by Larry Foster, General Whale

totally false. Panic breaks out among some misinformed people at the sight of the orca, but there is no reason for it.

Still, there is no denying that the orca is a fierce combatant. Eyewitness reports exist of orcas attacking whales much larger than themselves. Whale lore is full of such stories. In some the orca wins the battle, in some he loses. Various accounts survive from the old days of whaling, and of those certain tales are particularly credible. One careful observer was Frank T. Bullen, whose *Cruise of the Cachalot* was mentioned earlier. He reported seeing several instances of two orcas attacking either side of a sperm whale's mouth while a third orca worried the whale at the back. In one such case, the orcas won, apparently wanting only the tongue—a delicacy to the attackers. Bullen recorded another incident, validated by more contemporary and scientific observations, in which three or four orcas attacked a larger whale and got thoroughly trounced. Bullen said one orca he watched landed on the back of a sperm whale and was squashed by the huge descending fluke. The killer whale—and I much prefer the term orca—is therefore a whale killer, but he is not a *mankiller*; more precisely he is a cannibal.

Most writers who treat this subject say they know of no instance in which an orca has killed a human. I have read of only one such incident. This orca did not kill for food or because it habitually attacked humans; apparently the killing was an instance of calculated revenge. Dr. Paul Spong, a New Zealand psychologist who went to Vancouver to study orcas nearby, wrote about it in a paper reproduced in *Mind in the Waters*. He relates that in 1956 two loggers in British Columbia were sending logs down a steep embankment into the sea. One of the loggers thought it would be fun to aim some of the logs at a passing pod of orcas. A log hit one of the killer whales, hurting but not killing him. That night, as the two loggers were returning to their camp in their small boat, the orcas reappeared and tipped the boat over. The logger who had aimed the log at the passing orca was never seen again. The other man reached safety without incident.

F ossils show us what early animals, plants, birds, fish, and insects looked like. A number of scientific clues exist to tell us something of *Homo sapien*'s development, but there is much we do not know about our own evolution. The fact that so much of our own history is mere guesswork is one of many factors we have in common with the whales. As in our understanding of human evolution, missing links—unrecorded stages in development—make our knowledge of whale evolution incomplete. For example, no fossils or other remains exist to demonstrate the specific vital change from prehistoric whales (*Archaeoceti*) to modern whales.

The evidence we do have about the evolution of the whale shows us that a form of whale life came onto land as it developed four legs with which to negotiate its new, solid environment. This four-legged animal was most closely related to today's ungulates—cows and camels, for instance. According to Everhard Slijper in *Whales and Dolphins*, however, though a relationship with ancient cows and camels did exist, we should not conjure up pictures of a cow-like whale. The terrestrial ancestor was a very different animal, a carnivore (meat-eater) which eschewed vegetation. At its most ancient stage, it was an insect-eating carnivore, Slijper says.

For whatever reason, sometime over the eons, this terrestrial beast chose to return to the sea. When it began to readapt to the sea it evolved the most wonderful shape ever to develop in an all-marine environment. The forelegs changed into front flippers, and the hind legs disappeared completely—as far as can be seen from the outside. Because sound travels better and faster through the water, the ancient whale no longer needed external ears with which to collect sound from the air—yet buried in the flesh where the now-absent ears would have been found are the muscles for those lost ears! Everything external has been accommodated within the whale's body, leaving the outside perfectly streamlined—a torpedo-like tube that can move smoothly through the water with nothing left on it to create drag. There are no outside ears; and the genitals and mammary glands are located within slits in the skin. When the male is aroused, his penis becomes erect and pushes out of the slit. When the baby wants milk from his mother, he pushes against her mammary slit and forces the milk out. This milk is so rich it is as thick as cream.

When all systems are "go," the cetacean body is of the smoothest design imaginable. The powerful flukes, which are a cartilagenous extension over the defunct pelvis, can push the giant body along at amazing speeds. One diver who, by remarkable luck, was able to watch a humpback whale start from underwater and breach told me that it took

As this humpback whale breaches, the grooves on its belly become visible.

only two or three thrusts of the flukes to propel that forty-five-ton body completely out of the water!

Some clues to the whale's early land form can be found in the fetus of the modern whale. In the very young embryo, the hind legs are distinctly present and remain in some species up to about the eighth month of the gestation. (Gestation varies according to species from ten to sixteen months.) And within the flippers, even after birth, the inner bones show clearly, appearing much like arms, wrists, and fingers—more human in shape than one would expect of a relative, however distant, of the cow. One more animated demonstration of evolution occurs during gestation: When the whale once more evolved into a sea creature, the nostrils receded from the snout back to the top of the head so that the animal could breathe easily while moving horizontally through the water. In the early embryo, the nostrils are still at the top of the head; they travel backwards during the embryonic development so that they are in their blow hole position by the time the fetus is ready for birth.

When it returned to the sea, the ancient whale was long and slender; the descriptions I have read remind me of drawings of sea serpents and sea monsters. If it is true, as some believe, that the occasional "dragons" slain in Great Britain "in the days of old, when knights were bold" were not dragons but the last of the dinosaurs, then who is to say that until a couple centuries ago a few ancient whales did not survive to be mistaken as serpents or monsters? After all, in 1938, off the coast of Madagascar, a live coelacanth was caught—a fish which supposedly had become extinct 70 million years ago.

Speculation aside, this ancient whale looked almost snake-like, but had the cetacean flukes, the short, stubby fingers up forward, and the streamlined torpedo head. As various kinds of whales evolved, they gathered girth because they no longer had to maintain body proportions and weight which could be supported by legs.

Among the mysteries which may not be solved until the cetacean missing link is found is the matter of teeth. Scientists feel certain that the most ancient whales were baleen whales. Yet in the whale embryo, even the baleen whales today have tooth buds. Sometimes these buds are not overtaken by the beginnings of baleen until the eighth month of an eleven-month pregnancy. Today, among the great whales only the sperm whale has teeth, and then only on the lower jaw. Rudiments of teeth in the sperm's upper jaw remain buried in cavities which receive

The Humpback Whale

In this remarkable photograph, by Kenneth Balcomb, the left side of the whale's face is seen. This whale was guessed to be 35 feet long and weighing over 28 tons. Humpbacks are the most active and playful of whales.

Drawing by Larry Foster, General Whale

Flipper
A 45-foot Humpback may have flippers 14 feet long. The Humpback's flippers are the largest of all whales.

Dorsal fin
In some whale species the dorsal fins are distinctive. Humpbacks have a rather small, irregular dorsal fin, compared to closely related types (known as rorquals), which have a larger, sickle-shaped fin. Other whale species have no dorsal fin at all.

Tail flukes
A whale propels itself with powerful up strokes of the tail, which is horizontal. Humpback flukes have distinctive scalloped edges with swept-back tips. The contours of whale tails are uncommonly subtle and handsome in form.

Chin
The lower jaw protrudes slightly ahead of the upper jaw. There is a fleshy protuberance on the chin of unknown purpose.

Throat
Although it is commonly believed that the throat of the Humpback whale is a puffed up and rotund affair, this view shows the throat area is actually concave, making the animal quite streamlined.

Blowholes
Being mammals these creatures breathe no water. Whales breathe air. The nostrils have evolved to the top of the whale's head as an adaptation to the totally aquatic environment.

Eye
The eyes of whales are small. Water transmits sound in such excellent fashion that whale hearing has become astonishingly acute. The need to respond visually is greatly diminished, hence, small eyes.

Size
Humpbacks are not among the largest of whales. Humpies only reach lengths of 48 feet and weigh a mere 35 tons, while the Blue whale, the largest creature of all time, can attain lengths of 100 feet and weights of 130 tons.

the lower teeth when the mouth is shut. The tusk of the narwhal is a lone tooth, so this animal qualifies as an Odontoceti, too. The smaller whales, such as the orca, and the little whales, such as dolphins and porpoises, have teeth in quantity. If they all have a common ancestor, at what point —and why—did one group develop teeth, and other retain baleen?

With respect to the nose area in general, you may hear and be confused by the word *rostrum* if you spend any time at all in whalewatching circles. Rostrum means beak, such as birds have. It may seem improbable that whales have anything at all in common with birds. However, to refer to the front part of a whale's head as the nose is incorrect. The nose is actually composed of the blow holes on the top of the head. I have already hinted at the advantages of this topside location: The whale doesn't get a snootful of water when he dives or travels forward, and he can stick his blow holes above the water's surface to breathe without having to expose his whole head. The whale's rostrum, then, is that part of the head located in front of the nose—the blow holes —just as the beak of a bird is located in front of the nostrils.

Some of the wildest misstatements about whales come about through a misunderstanding of how whales breathe. Whales are not fish, and therefore they do not take in oxygen through the gills. They are mammals, and breathe air through their nostrils just as humans do. Two fascinating aspects of whale breathing are the so-called spout, more accurately called the blow; and the lungs, particularly as they relate to sounding (diving).

Whales do not purposely take in water any more than humans do when they breathe. Therefore, the substance we can see being emitted from a whale's blow holes is not water, as the word spout itself mistakenly suggests. Nor is it the condensation of breath we see on a cold day. A thorough explanation of the blow would require a scientific and anatomical discussion beyond the intent of this book. But a workable understanding of the phenomenon is not difficult to reach.

The whale does not take in the tremendous lungs-full of air that one might suppose, because the lungs, as compared to the body, are not all that large. Instead, what air that is expelled when the whale surfaces is pushed with a tremendous force through a very small nasal passage.

Thus, the air being breathed out is greatly compressed. When the air is suddenly free of the duct and therefore the whale's body, it expands suddenly and cools, producing the cloud of vapor we can see. The blow can be seen even in warm tropical air. In most of my whale photos a blow is visible to some degree. In some photos it is so thin it looks like an imperfection in the printing of the picture, because the water or horizon can be seen through it. Where the photo was taken almost simultaneously with the whale's emergence from the water, however, and therefore almost at the same instant he exhaled, the blow is thicker and is more opaque.

The shape of the blows differs from one species of whale to another, both because of the varying sizes of whales and the fact that some have one blow hole while others, such as the humpback, have two. Nevertheless, the blow of the humpback forms a single "cloud" over the head, while others, such as that of the right whale, produce two separate columns. The old whalers could tell at great distances which whale they had come across just by the characteristic of the blow.

Paul Budker, in *Whales and Whaling*, quotes authorities who contend that mucus and body oil are also expelled in the blow. I can accept the mucus idea, but the expulsion of oil in the blow seems to me impossible. The importance of whale oil in the old days seems to have overridden everything and has even carried over to permeate modern thinking. The whale is not so full of oil that he continually oozes it through his breath or anyplace else. Those who have watched whales sound notice that they leave behind them what has been called a "footprint." This is a large, round, flat expanse of water which forms over the point at which the whale leaves the surface. It was long held that this pattern was water becalmed by oil left behind when the whale sounded. Modern observations have proved this explanation to be false. The footprint is, of course, the result of the tremendous upward thrust of the whale's flukes as he dives; the force displaces water upwards and backwards, leaving the round flat area to dissipate slowly as it floats backwards from the location where the whale went under.

As mentioned, the whale's lungs are quite small in proportion to the rest of its body. The lungs of the large whales are, proportionally speaking, approximately half the size of an adult human being's lungs (though some dolphins and porpoises have lungs twice that relative size). The obvious question here is, Why aren't whales subject to the same limita-

Drawing by Larry Foster, General Whale

*In the Southern hemisphere minke whales have no white patch
on the flipper, as do the northern varieties.*

tions that human divers suffer? For example, why don't whales suffer
from crushed lungs under the tremendous pressure of deep water? And
why do they not contract the bends as would human divers who surfaced as quickly as whales do? As we shall see, the whales' bodies developed special adaptations to combat these pressure-related problems as
they evolved to adjust to their marine environment.

The sperm whale is a particularly impressive diver, and provides a
good example of the extent to which whales adapted to deep-water diving as they evolved. Because of the relative shallowness in the Maui-
Lanai area, sperm whales are rarely seen in this region even though they
do come within two hundred miles of the Islands. Therefore, my knowledge of their diving behavior is not first-hand. But the sperm is beautiful-
ly described by Victor B. Scheffer in his book *The Year of the Whale.* There
Scheffer explains that the sperm does not need to migrate to shallow
water to give birth. But the main reason the sperm whale remains in
deeper waters is that its chief food—the giant squid—is found there.

The bodies of sperm whales are often covered with marks from battles with the giant squid, battles which the sperm appears to be accustomed to winning. Sperm whales are helped by the fact that their teeth are pointed backwards, so they can hold their prey and prevent it from escaping. Bullen, in *Voyage of the Cachalot*, brilliantly describes a moonlit battle between a squid and sperm which he witnessed while he was on watch. Squid and sperm erupted from the ocean from who knows what depths, the squid's great tentacles wrapped every whichway around the whale, holding the latter in what appeared to be an impossible situation. But once the whale's teeth hit the vital spot, the squid was doomed.

Elsewhere, Paul Budker quotes from Robert Clarke, who wrote in *The Norwegian Whaling Gazette*, Number 10 (1955) that on July 4 of that year he was at the Azores when a sperm whale was taken, and in its stomach was found intact a squid measuring thirty-four feet in length, including the tentacles. The sperm whale itself measured forty-seven feet.

The sperm whale must dive to very great depths in pursuit of the giant squid, which brings us back to the question of lung size. As we will see with respect to cetacean brains, the size of an organ does not necessarily indicate its capacity. In this case, the relatively small lungs do not restrict the diving capabilities of the great whales. In fact, as indicated, the reverse is true. Sperm-whale remains have been found tangled in under-sea telephone and telegraph cables at depths of a half-mile and more. In *Home Is the Sea: For Whales*, Riedman and Gustafson relate that in 1932, a sperm carcass was discovered 3,500 feet below the surface. Six other sperms, they wrote, have been found at 450 fathoms—roughly a half-mile. Slijper records finds of sperm whales tangled in cables as deep as 3,000 feet.

How can the sperm whales dive to these depths with such small lungs? Cetologists explain that, to begin with, the whales are not made of "crushable" bodies. Thus the lungs are protected from the increasing water pressure by the whale's body itself. Also, the lungs are not the only place in which oxygen is stored. In the case of the deep-diving whales, a very small amount of oxygen is kept for the dive in the lungs, while the majority goes to the blood and the muscles. The especially high hemoglobin content of the cetaceans' blood is another deep-dive adaptation; it allows their blood to carry more oxygen. Cetaceans also have the ability to cut off blood circulation to parts of the body not needed during a dive so that most of the circulation occurs in the brain. And, finally, whales' muscles have the ability to go without air longer than do man's.

Shallenberger tells me that he has experienced some frustration in his work at Sea Life Park because of the cetacean ability to voluntarily vaso-constrict—that is, they can close off the blood flow of a given blood vessel at will. He says that when researchers need a blood sample from one of their dolphins, they take it from the tail area. The dolphins learned this quickly and often cut off the blood flow to the tail so that a blood sample could not be taken!

Although dolphins' lungs are somewhat larger than those of the greater whales relative to body size, these animals also have deep-diving body adaptations, such as this ability to shut off blood flow temporarily to non-essential body areas. Ordinarily, most dolphins appear to have little need to dive as deeply as, say, the sperm whale. They appear to do most of their feeding within seventy-five feet of the surface. They do sometimes feed, however, in the deep scattering layer at one thousand feet. The U.S. Navy, taking advantage of this deep-diving capacity, has engaged in some activities which are not thoroughly approved of by cetacean-lovers. They have trained dolphins to retrieve objects on the ocean floor—perhaps at the site of a sunken ship or submarine, or a stranded diver—at depths of more than a thousand feet.

The larger the animal—land or sea—the slower the breathing rate. On the average, human beings can hold their breath for about one minute if they must. Trained divers, such as Japanese pearl divers, can hold their breath for three minutes. Some experts say that the normal surface breathing rate for the great whales is one breath every two minutes. In a dive, however, the different whales have developed the ability to hold their breath for varying lengths of time. The time depends on the need of the specific whale. For instance, the sperm whale must dive deep, and perhaps fight for a long time, under water; the sperm has therefore developed the ability to hold the breath up to an hour and a half. The baleen whales, however, do not have to dive as far for krill, plankton, or small fish. Thus baleen whales have never developed the ability to hold breath as long as do the sperm whales. The need is not there. Plankton and krill are sometimes found at the surface; when the sun is high, it sinks like a cloud no more than 150 feet or so. The small fish can be at 100 feet in depth, but may require an underwater chase. I have timed the humpbacks to remain under for some 18 minutes. The length of time may have been occasioned by feeding, or by an attempt to stay out of sight of our boat. Others report that the humpback can remain under some 25 minutes. In any case, the feeding habits of the whale have determined the length of time that individual kinds of whale can remain under.

O ne final note regarding general whale physiology: The whale's average body temperature is 96 degrees Fahrenheit—not too far off from our optimum body temperature. The whale can withstand the cold Arctic and Antarctic waters because of its blubbery insulation. However, whales, including the "little whales"—dolphins and porpoises—do suffer from many of the same ailments humans do. Whales have been known to have pneumonia, diabetes, stomach ulcers, heart diseases, and tumors. One other condition shared with humans is worm infestation, and some cetologists believe that this ailment is the true explanation for the mysterious whale beachings that occur periodically— when one or several whales wash up on the shore and slowly die on land for no apparent reason. The theory goes that parasitic infestation gets into the brain or the ear of the whales and drive them mad, destroying their sense of direction or equilibrium. Some cetologists have attempted to pass the strange beachings off as demonstrations of a death wish or suicide attempt. This hypothesis seems unlikely to me, since the animals' own reasoning would tell them that land is the source of the air they must breathe. They would be setting themselves up for a prolonged and tortuous death through exposure to the sun by throwing themselves on the shore. As a matter of fact, the most efficient means of suicide would be drowning. Still, the cetacean brain has not yet been proved to possess the capability necessary to reach this conclusion.

S ome eighty different species of whales, porpoises, and dolphins exist on this planet. To name and describe all of them is outside the scope of this book; such information can be found in a textbook. This effort deals for the most part with cetaceans the reader has a chance of seeing, in the wilds on whalewatching excursions, or in seaquariums such as Marineland of the Pacific (near Palos Verdes, Los

Angeles), Sea World (San Diego, near Los Angeles), and Sea Life Park (Oahu).

The most commonly seen whales in the wild are the California (or Pacific) gray and the humpback whale. The orca is seen frequently and the pilot whale is sighted on occasion in the wild—both are commonly referred to as whales although both are, strictly speaking, the largest of the dolphins. In seaquariums the most frequently seen whales are the orca and the pilot. Among the smaller cetaceans, the bottlenose dolphin is the most often seen in captivity. Some seaquariums have other types of dolphins and porpoises, including the spinner. For example, Oahu's Sea Life Park has two rough-toothed dolphins, a rarity. The younger one was obtained during the rescue of a pod of seventeen which beached themselves on the island of Maui in July, 1976. Nine died, seven were successfully returned to the sea, and one was kept in captivity.

On the other end of the spectrum in terms of accessibility to the whale-watcher is the blue whale, which, because it grows to 100 feet and can weigh 150 tons, has been hunted more intensely and killed more methodically than any other whale. Speaking in terms of bulk, one blue could be worth six humpbacks to a whaler. When it was still "legal" to kill blue whales, as many as 30,000 per season were slaughtered in the Antarctic, where reliable whaling records have been kept since 1929. Records were not systematically kept in Arctic whaling, so it is not known how many blues were killed annually in the North. Until recently, it was thought that the blue whale had been wiped clean from the world's oceans. But in the last few years a few have been sighted here and there, mostly in the polar regions, both north and south. Two or three years ago, Jacques Yves Cousteau astounded the world by filming remnants of the blue family in the North Pacific. And in 1975, one lone blue whale, very much off course but keeping company with some gray whales, was seen in Monterey Bay, California.

This traveling sociability is not entirely unheard of. With the exception of the orca, which makes its potential victims leery, members of the cetacean family get along together very well. They do sometimes travel together, the most common example being the occasional humpback family traveling with the California (or Pacific) gray whales between Alaska and Baja California.

Shapes and Sizes
Compared

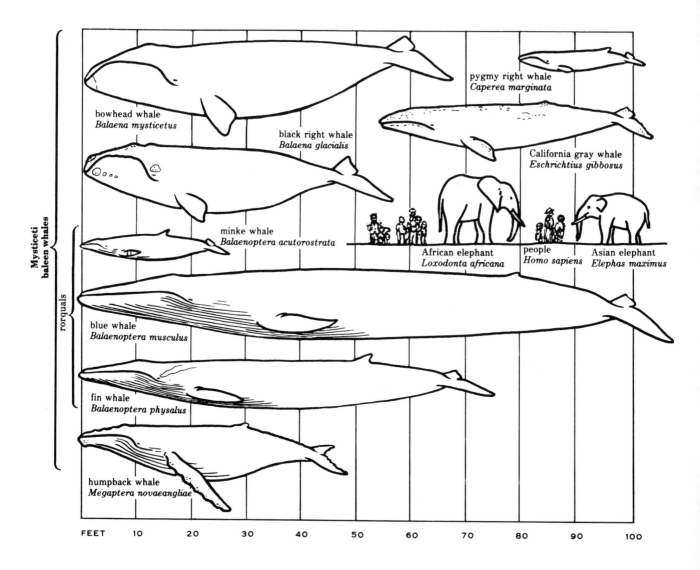

Mysticeti
baleen whales

rorquals

bowhead whale
Balaena mysticetus

black right whale
Balaena glacialis

pygmy right whale
Caperea marginata

California gray whale
Eschrichtius gibbosus

minke whale
Balaenoptera acutorostrata

African elephant
Loxodonta africana

people
Homo sapiens

Asian elephant
Elephas maximus

blue whale
Balaenoptera musculus

fin whale
Balaenoptera physalus

humpback whale
Megaptera novaeangliae

FEET   10   20   30   40   50   60   70   80   90   100

Drawing by Larry Foster, General Whale

There are 80 or so species of cetacea, i.e., whales, dolphins and porpoises. They are intelligent warm-blooded marine mammals with terrestrial ancestors, inhabiting all oceans of the world with several fresh water species living in rivers. They give live birth, nurse their young and show tenderness. And they breathe air, the nostrils having evolved to the top of the head. The skeletal structure is typically mammalian. For example, the basic bone structure of the cetacean flipper has the same bones as the human arm.

Little is known about whale life styles because the creatures have always been valued primarily as a raw material, rather than an object of natural science.

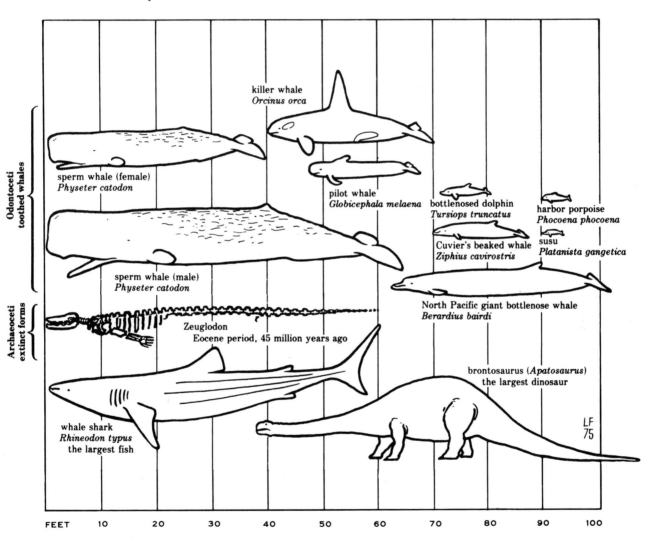

Odontoceti toothed whales

killer whale
Orcinus orca

sperm whale (female)
Physeter catodon

pilot whale
Globicephala melaena

bottlenosed dolphin
Tursiops truncatus

harbor porpoise
Phocoena phocoena

Cuvier's beaked whale
Ziphius cavirostris

susu
Platanista gangetica

sperm whale (male)
Physeter catodon

North Pacific giant bottlenose whale
Berardius bairdi

Archaeoceti extinct forms

Zeuglodon
Eocene period, 45 million years ago

brontosaurus (*Apatosaurus*)
the largest dinosaur

whale shark
Rhineodon typus
the largest fish

LF
75

FEET   10   20   30   40   50   60   70   80   90   100

The face of the blue whale.

Intelligence and Communication

To some it may appear that a layman such as myself dares to write about the brain and consciousness of cetaceans only out of egomania. This field of study is relatively new. It is a field in which there is still much more to be learned than is already known and understood. Investigations into such delicate and subtle areas can be made properly only by doctors of medicine or psychology. Therefore, when discussing facts and their meaning, I write only as a reporter, passing on information and conclusions that have been discovered and originated by others.

Still, it may be said that scientists theorize, but that amateur naturalists often fantasize—imagining something to be true because they *want* it to be true. Early on in the study of cetology, one hypothesis gained precedence and it is one that appealed to naturalists very much. The hypothesis is that cetaceans may be thinking and reasoning animals. The implications of this possibility are tremendous, for these capabilities have so far been detected only in *Homo sapiens*. After looking at the assembled facts known thus far, the photographs and diagrams made of cetacean brains, and the behavior and lifestyles of the animals themselves, it is impossible for me, at least, to doubt the veracity of some of the initial conclusions drawn by the experts which support the idea that cetaceans are reasoning animals. I find it equally impossible to doubt the conclusions which form in my own mind. I believe these animals can consciously assess a situation and decide on a course of action. I believe this because the evidence falls into place to support such a conclusion—both because I want it to, and because it has to.

I must confess that until recent years, I had only vague ideas that the whale was, in the first place, a fellow animal, and in the second place, something other than a dumb hulk of blubber. The real nature of whales only came home to me a couple of years ago, shortly after I had written a

story about them for my newspaper, *The Maui News*. The story concerned
the two federal laws which now protect cetaceans, the Marine Mammals
Protection Act and the Endangered Species Act. The crux of the article
was that the whales should not be killed because their numbers are
diminishing so rapidly. In response to the story I received a telephone
call from a young man who said he thought it was sad that the only
reason I advanced for the protection of whales was the fact they are being
killed to the verge of extinction.

The young man was James Hudnall. He has a B.A. in marine geology,
but became so fascinated with the whales of the ocean that he put the
ocean's rocks aside. He devoted his full energies to the study of cetaceans, and once having amassed enough information about them for a
base, he began using that data as a means of obtaining grants or jobs
which permit him to study the whales. With the world's interest in
whales mushrooming, and with their importance being appreciated
more and more, he is finding cetology a fertile field.

"Why should anyone have to give reasons for not killing any animal?"
he asked. And he later repeated the question when I invited him to
discuss his views with Lahaina's whalewatchers.

"I give one extremely important reason not mentioned [in *The Maui
News* story], a reason quite important in the thinking of many Mainland
conservationists who have spoken out against the slaughter of the whale:
the possible intelligence of the whales," he told us.

He emphasized the word, "possible," saying that it has not yet been
proved that whales can reason, but that much evidence indicates the
possibility.

"There is some point in man's relationships with other creatures where
he does not kill them, but instead he tries to communicate," Jim continued. "It is the point where we presume that the other creature is intelligent enough to understand and capable of answering back."

It was at this point that one of my seemingly unrelated mental flashes
struck me: How absurd we have been, reaching out to other planets and
other worlds in outer space in our search for intelligent life, when we
have intelligent life in our own "inner space," as the sea is called, which
we have ignored completely.

Hudnall told us at that meeting that there are two basic reasons why
those who study whales feel they are intelligent creatures: the nature of

their brains, and the nature of their behavior. The whale brain is phys-ically large, said Hudnall. The humpback's weighs eleven pounds, the sperm whale's weighs eighteen pounds, while the human brain weighs in at three pounds. However, qualified scientists have written that brain size does not tell the whole story in the measure of intelligence. Of these some say the size of the brain merely matches proportionally the size of the body it is in, but Hudnall and a number of scientists do not believe this to be an argument against cetacean intelligence. True, the human brain is larger with respect to body weight. The humpback's brain makes up .02 percent of his body weight; the bottlenose dolphin's brain, .225 percent; while our brain measures 1.93 percent of our body weight.

Hudnall's point is that since both animals have large brains, the key consideration is what has been happening to both brains during their evolution. Hudnall said researchers show that human beings have had a large (in terms of the rest of the human body) brain for about one million years. Whales have had their eleven- and eighteen-pound brains for 30 million years. Thus, what is important here is the difference in time the brains have had to evolve. The conclusion is not especially flattering to the human being. The whale's large brain has had 29 million more years to evolve!

Hudnall said that the brains of cetaceans "appear to be more integrated and more contemplative" than the humans' brain. "How do they express themselves?" we asked. "Observers say that they show more awareness."

Many of us have seen the "trained" dolphins at marine parks, such as Oahu's Sea Life Park, or Marineland in California. How trained are they? Those who work with them now prefer to say that they are *educated* as to what we expect of them, not *trained* the way a dog is. And Hudnall recited a favorite story which may prove that point. He recalled that cetacean researcher John Lilly was doing what we have seen "trainers" do at these marine parks—rewarding a porpoise with a fish every time the porpoise did what was asked of her. After a while, the porpoise had her fill of fish, but wanted to continue playing games, so she continued to accept a fish after each performance. Instead of eating them, however, she stacked the fish rather neatly at the bottom of the tank. Finally, the porpoise tired of playing, and to indicate this she went to the bottom of her tank, brought back up one of the fish, and "handed" it to Lilly as a reward!

S tudies have shown that cetacean brains are very similar to human brains except for two notable differences, which, to my thinking, actually make the cetacean brain superior to ours. The first difference has to do with the subtlety of perception. Human beings have five senses; they inform themselves about their environment through sight, sound, touch, taste, and smell. If one sense is lost another often becomes heightened. In fact, blind persons often appear to develop an entirely new sense. I hesitate to call this new capacity "compensatory," because it obviously does not make up for the loss of sight. But because sight is lost another awareness often develops—the ability to actually perceive the presence of something without seeing it. For example, blind people walking in a field can somehow sense that a tree is in front of them, blocking the way. They know approximately when to reach out and feel for it, so they can walk around it. It is sometimes possible for a fully sighted person to close the eyes and, to a limited degree, experience this sense.

I am not prepared to say whether this new capacity to perceive is what we like to call a "sixth sense," whether it is the result of listening more closely and thus actually "hearing" the presence of an object as we approach it sightless, or whether the mind has the undeveloped or subconscious facility to sense the presence of an object through the forehead—almost radar-like. Is the forehead acting like a radar shield, and is some part of the brain functioning as a radar screen? Or is the phenomenon merely due to a more acutely developed hearing sense?

The undeniable fact is, however, this usually untapped capacity does exist in humans, and when the need arises, it can be developed and refined. In cetaceans, however, this perceptual ability exists ready-made. Whales' eyes are on the sides of their heads. Therefore, they have two blind spots in their field of vision: one directly ahead, where vision is blocked by the huge head; one directly behind the whale, where vision is interrupted by the mass of the body. (The whalers of olden days took advantage of this fact and took care to approach a whale from directly astern; this way they hoped to be in position for a perfect strike with the harpoon before the whale noticed their presence.)

These deficiencies are not so pronounced in the smaller whales, especially the dolphins, but the blackout areas in the large whales are gigantic. And so, just as the nostrils traveled backwards on the head when the land cetacean evolved into the sea cetacean, so has this latent sense which we all share become highly developed in the cetacean to compensate for the blind area. One aspect of the capacity to perceive unseen objects is expressed in the cetacean's ability to "echolocate." Briefly put, this means that a cetacean locates an object, or learns how far ahead of him an object is, by emitting a sound into the blind area (or any area, for that matter), and mentally measuring the time the sound takes to travel from him, bounce off the object, and return. The role of a sound in performing this act is not well understood insofar as it concerns whales; the chances for study are almost nil. In porpoises and dolphins, however, echolocation has been studied and pretty much understood. Some seaquariums have "acts" to demonstrate the echolocating abilities of their dolphins. The large whales may activate their "radar" without emitting sounds themselves.

Without getting more technical, it is still possible to conclude that the human and cetacean brain have in common the ability to perceive unseen objects but that in the cetacean this capacity is much more highly refined than in the human.

As mentioned, there is a second area in which the cetacean brain and the human brain have similarities yet differ in capacity. The second distinction is more dramatic; because of it, I am convinced that the cetacean has a more sophisticated brain and a much richer appreciation of his environment than we do. The distinction is this: The cetacean brain has what is known as a paralimbic lobe, and the human brain does not. In the most simple terms, "para" means something that is alongside something else; and "limbic" means it is separate, distinct, with definite boundaries or borders. In other words, the paralimbic lobe is a separate lobe, or part of the brain—an additional part of the brain which cetaceans alone have. Because we humans do not have such a lobe it is difficult to explain in human terms what it is and what it does. In modern terms, the total effect might best be explained as that of a computer.

The cetacean's overall brain may be likened to the computer's memory bank. The whale enters into a situation and sizes it up with all his senses. The data gathered through the senses flash instantly through the paralimbic lobe, the heart of the computer, turning what the individual senses have perceived into one multifaceted perception. The whale is then completely immersed in one single sensation which we know only by perceiving its components—separate, one-at-a-time sensations. The whale instantly knows that which a human has to arrive at through inductive reasoning: What does it look like? What does it feel like? What does it sound like? What does all this add up to?

The cetacean brain, it may now be seen, is a fascinating thing to contemplate. When I first began to realize the meaning of its subtle differences, I thought of a discussion I once heard about muscular dystrophy: How awful it must be to have a brain that functions perfectly but be trapped inside a body over which you have no control! I wondered if this insight could relate to the whale. What would he do with this brain if he had arms and hands, legs and feet, and could walk on the earth? Is it proper to think of the whale as "condemned" to live in the water, with his limbs transformed into useless flippers and flukes? Somehow, I think not. I like to think that, as long as 25 million years ago, the whales realized something as a result of those built-in computers of theirs, something we humans have not yet stumbled upon. Earth's land area is getting crowded and its resources are disappearing. With the greater part of the earth's surface covered by water, where do you suppose the future lies?

What do you say, Brother Whale?

One of the things that amazes people upon their introduction to the cetacean family is the fact that these mammals make sounds and, through these sounds, they can communicate. In the case of the smaller whales—the dolphins and porpoises—these sounds are a series of whistles and clicks. Humans can hear some of these dolphin sounds, but the animals are capable of making these sounds at such a high frequency that they are out of our range of hearing. Humans can hear up to 15 or even 20 kilohertz; dolphins can make sounds, audible to each other, upwards to 150 kilohertz.

The larger the whale, the more sophisticated the sounds they make appear to be. At about the size of the pilot whale (more than 15 feet) cetaceans stop clicking and start making throatier, gutsier sounds. Also, whales have a deeper voice range than humans, so their voices can travel farther. The humpback of Hawaii's winter waters in particular have rich "voices," in which they utter what have been called "songs." One might consider use of that word an instance of anthropomorphizing, but Dr. Roger Payne, an expert on whale sounds, explains that the word "song" is used because the humpback makes many varied sounds which are uttered in complete sequences. The sequences are repeated sound for sound, again and again. Astonishingly, some of the sequences can last for twenty minutes. Payne gives this explanation on the jacket cover of his remarkable LP record, "Songs of the Humpback Whale." The recordings for the LP were made near Bermuda. He finds, as have other researchers, that the humpback songs change from year to year in the same geographical area and differ from one part of the world to another. It would seem, in human terms, as though the humpbacks have different languages in the different parts of their sea world just as we humans do on land. Payne noted some of these differences in sound patterns when we compared his recordings of humpbacks off Bermuda with the songs he heard in 1976 when he listened to the Maui humpbacks through a hydrophone. He has told friends that he hopes to come back in 1977 to set up what may become a permanent on-going study of the North Pacific humpbacks. A series of such studies could begin to crack the mystery of why the humpbacks of one ocean or one hemisphere so rarely mix with those of another region. It may also detect a link among the different "accents" or "languages."

But perhaps in referring to varying languages and dialects I am looking too closely for some ancient link between humans and cetaceans. I do feel there is a mystical link, if no other. And as I write about the whales, when I have stopped and then go back to face another blank sheet of paper, I turn on a tape I made of humpback songs and listen to them for a moment. Their voices, for some strange reason, never fail to propel my mind back into the world of the whale, and the writing business at hand!

Some cetologists believe that different species of whales can and do communicate with each other, actually "talk" with each other. Yet each species of whale has its own distinct sound. The "voice" of the humpback is, I believe, the most distinct and the most distinctive. Its range is from the very high, almost a squeak, to the very low, a basso profundo which we might expect a whale to have. And as with the sounds of all whales, researchers have shown that the songs—or stories, or conversations, or whatever you wish to call them—of the humpbacks are delivered at tremendous speeds. Recordings of them can be slowed down so that it becomes apparent that thousands of syllables and "words" are uttered in a second. Kenneth S. Norris, in his book *The Porpoise Watcher*, refers to the dolphin talk as "rusty-hinge sounds," and says instruments measuring these sounds made by Kathy, a bottlenose dolphin with whom he worked, revealed "hundreds of tiny clicks, each about a thousandth of a second long." Payne has stated that the sounds of the larger whales are even more complex.

There is obviously intelligence behind this activity. It is unlikely that the complex songs of the humpback are instinct and they cannot be habit. At the other extreme of possibilities is the most anthropomorphic fantasy of all: One can be tempted to look at the whales, their "hands" now fused by evolution into flippers which can grasp nothing (let alone a pen!), and recall that before writing was invented, and even now in places where illiteracy prevails, people remembered historical events by putting them into verse. Could the whale be reciting ballads? The cetologists have not yet proved this to be a foolish notion. I prefer to consider it a possibility. I would hate to accept the interpretation that the songs of the humpbacks are nothing more than sound-alikes as are the songs of the birds!

Just as the rich variety of the humpback recitations makes that cetacean sound dignified, so the chatter of the little porpoises and dolphins sounds light-hearted and gossipy. To another dolphin or porpoise, however, it is as significant as the stentorian tones in the song of one humpback to another. The little guys, however, seem more playful, and it is easy to imagine that their talk is frivolous, too.

I was recently delighted to hear of an experience gleefully recounted to me by David Russell, a charter boat captain who works out of Lahaina. He had taken a group to Manele Bay, on the island of Lanai, a sail of just under two hours from Lahaina. His passengers walked with crewmen to nearby White Manele, as the beach area is called, but Captain Russell elected to remain behind with the boat. The harbor is small, and sometimes it's necessary for a visiting boat to move so that residents can get in or out.

From the deck of his boat he looked out over the breakwater and saw six or eight dolphins swimming, leaping, and otherwise playing around only about ten yards away. He said they looked as though they were having so much fun that he donned face mask and snorkle and jumped in to join them. A very young dolphin kept coming up to within four feet of him, and they stared at each other nose-to-nose. All the while the little one made a series of "beep beep" sounds that, the captain said, sounded exactly like the Roadrunner of cartoon movie fame. The other dolphins stayed farther away, but kept circling around and around, watching him closely, for about half an hour. "They kept up this continual line of chatter," he said. "They must have all been women dolphins!"

Hopefully, the chauvinistic remark can be excused, in exchange for a first person account of a romp with what Dr. Lilly has referred to as "the humans of the sea."

Divers in the Lahaina area tell me that they always know when it is whale season. Even if they can't see the whales, they can hear them. Estimates as to how far one whale can hear another's voice vary. It is generally agreed that they can converse with each other at a distance of twenty-five to thirty miles easily, for the water acts as a natural sound conductor. Some researchers believe that they have picked up humpback songs on their hydrophones from as far away as seventy-five miles. And several cetologists are currently at work on a theory that one whale can hear another one three hundred miles away. The question has even been raised whether a humpback in the Arctic can talk with a humpback in the seas off Greenland, since the voice could carry that distance in the water under the ice pack? Cautiously some scientists are admitting, "It appears to be possible."

Those who hear the cetaceans are always excited, and many times they find themselves amazed. Jim Hudnall tells of a day he spent off Maui shortly after he learned to mimic the dolphin chatter. He doesn't know whether or not he was actually "saying" anything, but he did obtain response. Dolphins came to look at him, and while he was mimicking them he heard the unmistakable booming sound of a humpback. Apparently attracted by his cetacean vocalizations, a fullgrown humpback whooshed into view, slowed down long enough to look at Hudnall and the dolphins, then swooshed on through the underwater scene and out of sight. Jim says that he was too excited to think of being frightened. Ever since then, although he has been very close to fullgrown humpbacks, even cow whales with very young calves—so close that the baby's entire body would not fit into the viewing frame of his camera—he says he has never known fear of them.

This lack of fear is generally expressed by other divers I have talked with. One I spoke with two and three years ago was Bud Hedrick, formerly of Lahaina but now a Sausalito resident. At the time he was skipper of the schooner *Mayan*, owned by rock star David Crosby. Bud was an avid Scuba diver and underwater photographer during those years in Lahaina. He recalled the first time he encountered a humpback cow and calf: "There were about four adults ahead of me and the baby. It was pretty dark at that depth, and I wanted to get closer to take photos. I got as close as I dared, and I never really felt afraid of them. I just didn't want to upset the mother. I wasn't sure what I should do, how close I should get. But just then one of the adult whales answered the question for me. Up he came, almost fifty feet of him, and he stopped within a yard of my mask. He just hovered there for a moment, then he let out these deep, booming sounds. He was telling me to lay off. After giving me the word, he slowly turned around and rejoined the others. I knew where my place was, and I stayed there and watched. They stayed where they were for a while, fussing around the new baby and giving him all sorts of attention. Then, they slowly moved off. It was almost insulting, because after that one bull had told me off, they never again paid any attention to me."

Migration

One way of becoming familiar with whale behavior and life cycles is to study the great annual migrations. In the course of such study, it will soon become clear why the gray and humpback whales—the ones most often seen by the nonprofessional whalewatcher —are considered by many to be the most interesting of the great whales.

First, you must remember that summer and winter take place at opposite times of the year in the northern and southern hemispheres of the globe. Most whales take part in some sort of migration every year, and the journeys tend to correspond with changes in season. When it is coldest and when the ice pack is solid in the polar regions where they feed, the whales travel to warmer waters. When the polar thaw begins, the whales return.

The natural migration cycle appears to depend on two factors: the availability of food and the point reached in the mating and birthing cycle. With respect to the food factor, krill, the tiny, shrimp-like animals on which the gray and humpback whales thrive, are found in the world's cold waters because their own food is most plentiful there. However, during the winter when the ice extends farther into the open sea, the whales are no longer able to "harvest" the krill through their huge baleen strainers; the tiny prey are simply inaccessible. Until recently, it appeared that for the several months spent in their warm-water habitat, the whales did not eat anything except an occasional snack to kill the rumbles in the stomach. Observers often remark that when the whales return from the warm waters they tend to be noticeably thinner than when they left.

Lately, however, new evidence has begun to suggest that the baleens' fasts may not be so rigorous. Earlier we discussed the baleen whales' ventral grooves, which allow the throat and stomach to expand or contract like an accordian. Jim Hudnall, the man who had a significant effect on my own awareness of the nature of whales, has photographed humpbacks off Maui with their throats expanded like a bullfrog's, a clear demonstration of the fact that we are still adding to our knowledge of the daily habits of whales. Hudnall's sightings seemed to contradict the hypothesis that the humpbacks do not eat at all while in their warm-water calving and mating grounds. They could also have a bearing on the belief that humpbacks live exclusively on krill and plankton, and that they probably do not eat fish at all.

Hudnall's photos do not actually prove that the humpbacks were eating fish, but the physical appearance of the whales in the pictures indicates that they were eating *something*. There is plankton in Hawaiian waters, although not in the abundance it is found in colder waters. Marine biologists have observed, again in Hawaiian waters, that this free-floating microscopic animal matter sinks deep in the water as the sun gets higher, and rises close to the surface at night, early morning, and late afternoon, when the sun is low or beneath the horizon. Therefore, plankton is available for the humpbacks to eat during their Hawaiian visit. It would be difficult to imagine the humpbacks deliberately choosing to fast in the presence of this food supply.

As to whether the humpback whales eat small fish, this is plausible, although not conclusively proved for the scientific record. Other baleen whales, such as the finbacks about which Farley Mowat writes, have already been seen to eat herring. In a talk he gave at the January 1976 meeting of the Maui Chapter of the American Cetacean Society, Hudnall made a case for his hypotheses: "Baleen whales were thought to feed only on krill. They also feed on small fish. Just recently it was documented that they are feeding on herring off Alaska.

"In order to feed on herring, they use a very interesting technique. It consists of the whale blowing bubbles which formed more or less of a net for the herring. The herring were afraid to go through the bubbles. This enabled the humpbacks to then capture the herring in their mouth.

"I don't know whether humpbacks eat in Hawaiian waters or not. I would suspect they do. . . . Every once in a while you'll find a humpback whale, and there'll also be a school of fish, and with the humpbacks right there in the middle, you wonder what they are doing with those schools of fish."

The bubbles left behind by humpbacks sparkle, and they may well appear to be a solid barrier to fish trying to swim through them. Thus the

The mating game: All is quiet as two humpbacks, flippers partially extended, snuggle.

And then the splashing starts!

fish may behave as if they are trapped inside a kind of corral that a circling whale describes. Farley Mowat, in *A Whale for the Killing*, describes another feeding strategy, used by the fin whales he observed, and I believe the humpbacks could use this method, too, if they were in a situation where they had to "herd" their intended meal rather than just swimming into a school of fish head on. The undersides of several species of whales are white. This group includes humpbacks, fin whales, and blue whales (the latter thereby nicknamed "sulphur bottom"). Mowat has watched the finners circle around a school of herring with increasing speed, herding them into a tight cluster because, again, the continuous circling motion gives the fish the impression that they are surrounded. In this instance, the impression comes from the light reflecting off the white of the whale's underside until, as the whale circles faster and faster, it appears to be a solid white band—a net or fence around them. Once the fish are convinced that they are surrounded, the whale dashes in open-mouthed for the Big Gulp! The white on the underside of the humpback may serve the same purpose. The field is wide open for humpback watchers to bring in some solid evidence to confirm the fish-eating theory.

At any rate, once the krill become unavailable, the whales head for tropical and subtropical areas, but not, apparently, to look for food. Instead they are seeking warmer and shallower water. These more comfortable conditions are necessary for mating and calving—as explained earlier, the whales mate one year and calve the next. The newborn whale does not have a protective layer of blubber to act as a shield from the cold. Also, once the baby is born, it must be pushed to the surface immediately so it can take its first breaths of air. If it breathes water, it will drown just like any other mammal. Obviously, this is another reason for birthing in warm waters. The whales cannot risk being trapped under the winter ice of the Arctic or the Antarctic: they must surface to breathe.

In order to get an overall view of the migrations, picture a globe of the earth in your mind. The whales move across the planet in a uniform up and down pattern—north and south—no matter what part of the globe you concentrate on. When it is winter in the southern hemisphere, the whales of the southern hemisphere are moving northward toward the tropics. At the same time, it is summer in the northern hemisphere, so the whales of the northern hemisphere are also migrating north, away from the tropics and back to the cold but now ice-free waters where the food is. And for the babies, born in the warm waters, this is a first-time trip.

Looked at in this overall manner, the migration pattern itself demonstrates why the whales of the north and the whales of the south rarely mix. They are hardly ever in the middle of the globe at the same time; thus they don't meet up with their relatives from the opposite hemisphere to exchange news.

But whales do live in most of the world's oceans, though their numbers are now sadly diminished, so these seasonal journeys are taking place all over the world. And groups of whales tend to travel between the same two general regions. For example, there are six different "neighborhoods" in Antarctic waters. These neighborhoods are large; they take up thousands of square miles of ocean. The whales who live in the Antarctic waters south of, say, Australia and New Zealand habitually visit the waters of Australia and New Zealand during their yearly migrations north. Other whale stocks go only from Antarctica to waters off South America. Still others go north to South Africa, and some travel as far north as the seas off Arabia.

In the course of historical inquiries, a change, small but significant, has been noted in the migrations of some whales. The changes appear to have taken place during the past four hundred years, and many believe that they are due to centuries of whaling activity. As we saw earlier, whales were originally hunted from shore stations. As the numbers of whales near shore decreased, the whalers took to boats. Those who argue that whaling has detered migration routes believe not that the coastal whales were killed off, but rather that the whales comprehended the situation and stayed further out to sea.

One whale which was once plentiful but now all but gone is the black, or Biscay, right whale. The Bay of Biscay, from which this right whale gets its name, is the bay bordering the Basque country of northern Spain and southern France—the home of the first whalers. At one time, the whalers thought that all the Biscay right whales had been killed off. But in their search for other whales out on the high seas, they found that the remnant of the Biscay right whale population was avoiding coastal waters. Needless to say, these whales soon found themselves in a "no place to hide" situation, and they became so scarce that they are now on the

International Whaling Commission's "protected" list. Thus can human activity influence the natural history of our planet.

The Greenland right whale, also called the bowhead whale, remains pretty much in northern waters, moving little most of the year. They are found not only off Greenland, but also off northern Pacific Russia. The great blue whale usually does not travel too far, nor does the unique narwhal, he of the great long tusk; they stay in Arctic waters and move only slightly to accommodate the annual increase in ice cover. By contrast, another baleen whale, Bryde's whale, tends to stick to the warm waters of the world year round. He is somewhat the exception in the tropics, as are the blue, narwhal, and fin in the Arctic. The fin whales travel, but do not migrate the vast distances most of the rest do. In recent years, blue whales have become more common off California.

Rather than getting into a whale-by-whale migration discussion, this account will concentrate on the migration patterns of the North Pacific humpbacks and gray whales, whales which people close to the Pacific Ocean have a chance to observe. Both the humpbacks and the grays spend the warmer half of the year in northern Pacific waters. Both are baleen whales, but the gray does not have the dorsal fin that the humpback has—that is, the humpback is a rorqual but the gray is not. The humpback whale averages 45 to 50 feet in length, while the gray tends to be 4 or 5 feet shorter. As noted earlier, once in a while a humpback family will migrate with the grays, but the reverse, to the best of my knowledge, has never been recorded. At this point, we know much more about the gray whale than about the humpback. In fact, more appears to have been learned about the humpback in the last two or three years than has been known altogether in the past.

Both species conform to the code obeyed by the rest of the migrating whales: They leave their cold North Pacific summer homes to spend winter in more hospitable climates. The gray whales apparently are divided into two stocks, the California and the Korean. The California grays migrate down the western North American coast, while the Korean grays travel down the Pacific coast of Russia. The humpbacks head south to Hawaii.

The grays and the humpbacks start their migrations south at the same time. Every November, the grays start their coastal trip, while the humpbacks head out to the open sea. There is not even a theory as to why the two take different courses. The humpback is known to be the most gregarious of the whales; it mingles freely with the grays in Alaskan waters in the summer. Come mating and calving season, however, and it takes its separate path.

As the grays head down the Pacific Coast, whalewatchers in British Columbia, Washington, Oregon, and California head for their favorite shore stations to watch the passing parade. At Point Loma, near San Diego, the National Park Service has even set up an official whalewatching station. The grays swim on in large family groups, heading south of California to Mexico's Baja California and their winter destinations. One stopping point is Scammon's Lagoon, named for the old Yankee whaler who first discovered this breeding ground. The other is San Ignacio Lagoon. (The Mexican government has declared Scammon's a whale sanctuary and prohibits boats from entering. Whalewatchers in boats can still enter San Ignacio.) Meanwhile, the humpbacks have headed to their breeding grounds in the waters between the islands of Maui, Molokai, Lanai, and Kahoolawe.

Viewing the gray whales is not at the optimum from the coasts of Washington and Oregon. The migration routes follow a pattern only in a general sense, and may be dictated both by food availability—if, indeed, they do eat while in migration—and by the existence of natural enemies. For example, the orcas found in the waters off southern British Columbia and northern Washington may keep the migrations out to sea several miles. Thus the passing of the grays along these northern coasts may be detected from the air, then witnessed by whalewatchers making the special trip out by boat.

Viewing off the California coast is better. It starts in late November, though sometimes not until December, and continues into January. The actual route varies, but appears to be influenced by California's coastal bulge. South of San Francisco and on to Baja California the whales come within easy sight of shore—sometimes as close as 500 yards at Point Pinos on the Monterey Peninsula, for instance.

The return back from Mexico to Alaskan waters can be spread out over a six-week period starting in late March. The pods of whales do not all sally forth at once like a Naval flotilla, but rather each pod reacts to its own family needs. This is usually dictated by the age of the newborn whales. Pods in which the babies arrived early are ready to return north earlier than others. Similarly, the departure from Alaska depends on both the food supply and the water temperature—both variables which can change a migration's start by as much as an entire month. The grays were three weeks "late" in 1975.

Needless to say, off both California and Hawaii the whalewatching-cruise business is increasing along with the growing interest in whales. From California, daily boat excursions go out to follow the grays. In the past four years (1972-76), the American Cetacean Society in cooperation with the Cabrillo Marine Museum in San Pedro has sponsored cruises for a total of 132,000 schoolchildren. Both boat and air cruises take whale-watchers to Baja California. The cruises are operated privately under increasingly strict governmental guidelines. (Controls on whalewatching will be discussed more fully in Chapter 6.)

Both the grays and the humpbacks start their return journey to the north in late March, the last of the families leaving the warm waters in early May. It has only recently been learned, in late summer of 1976 by a study team of the National Marine Fisheries Service, that the humpbacks, in addition to frequenting the more open sea areas such as the Bering Sea, also head for the protected inland waters of Alaska. This study, by the way, dovetails nicely into a study of humpbacks in Hawaiian waters being conducted by government biologists in the 1976-77 season. Hawaii may soon become a world center of whale study. The islands' two top cetologists, Dr. Tim Smith of the University of Hawaii and Dr. Edward W. Shallenberger, with the moral backing of such experts as Dr. Roger Payne of the New York Zoological Society, are working toward this end.

Because the grays' migration route has been well known for so long, whalers have never had any trouble finding these whales. Three times since the beginning of the nineteenth century, gray whales have been near extinction. First, in the late 1850s, they failed to appear at their usual coastal rendezvous off the Washington/British Columbia area, where the Indians traditionally waited to hunt them. Apparently, they learned the same lesson their brothers, the Biscay right whales, learned—they simply moved out to sea, out of sight of those who awaited them on shore. Unlike the Biscay right, which finally had no place to hide, the grays did make a comeback. It was during their resurgence that Captain Scammon learned their Mexican secret.

Forty tons of humpback, almost completely out of the water.

The second time the whalers reported a shortage of grays was in the period from about 1880 through the beginning of the 1920s. There were so few gray whales then that the whalers stopped hunting them altogether and went elsewhere for different species. The indiscriminant killing of calving mothers in Scammon's Lagoon apparently pushed the entire stock to the brink of extinction. The gray whales started a slow comeback when the whalers left them alone. When the hunting resumed, the gray whales once again diminished in numbers.

According to Riedman and Gustafson, in *Home Is the Sea: For Whales*, the last time the grays verged on extinction was around 1930, when the harpoons with explosive heads were first used to slaughter them. These writers recorded that only about one hundred grays were believed extant in 1935. In 1937, the gray whale was put on the protected list by the International Whaling Commission. They are now back in more healthy numbers.

The International Whaling Commission is rarely referred to in this book as the savior of the whales. The fact that the commission put the grays on its protected list had only a small part, if any, in their recovery. Many of the whaling nations are notorious for ignoring the rules they have agreed to abide by. The real reason the grays were not hunted as ruthlessly as before was not because whalers respected their protected status, but because the whalers knew that when a species becomes protected too few individuals are left to make the hunt profitable. From this reasoning a strategy emerged: Whalers would go to other ocean areas for other kinds of whales once a certain species appeared doomed. For this reason the humpback, now protected, appears to be holding its own. This may also be why the blue is once again being seen from time to time.

The greatest protection the grays receive now is from the American government, which has prohibited whaling since 1972 under the Marine Mammal Protection Act to be discussed more fully in Chapter 6. The Act applies only in American waters, of course, but that's where the grays are most highly visible. Now the Mexican government has joined in protecting the grays, at least in Scammon's Lagoon. A century ago, Captain Scammon, who wrote the first authoritative text on cetaceans (1874), readily admitted that his men killed baby whales in order to bait their mothers into becoming easier targets. But the mothers put up such horrendous defenses that the grays were called "devilfish" by the whalers, and this sobriquet stuck. Thus it has taken nearly a century to protect the baby "devilfish" that Scammon discovered being born. It is urgently to be hoped that saving the rest of the world's whales from slaughter will take considerably less time.

As a footnote to a discussion about migration patterns, we must give some attention to the resources which determine those patterns. Although the humpbacks frequent different territories and observe unseen boundaries which they rarely cross, each humpback stock has the same problems and goes about solving these problems in much the same manner. Feeding is perhaps the greatest task they have in common. Riedman and Gustafson write that the terrestrial ancestors of the whales apparently made their decision to return to the sea at a time when the population of the various land animals was increasing so rapidly that the active, daily competition for food had become more than the pre-whales wanted to cope with. Since the sea covers nearly three-quarters of the earth's surface, food was bound to be plentiful there.

Some thinkers believe that we should take a lesson from those prehistoric whale-ancestors. They conclude from the ever-diminishing state of the world's food supply that the only hope for the human race in the future is the farming of the sea. It is interesting to note that almost all these people—scientists, laypeople, and even science-fiction writers, who are sometimes a combination of the first two—do not limit their speculation to the existing foods of the ocean. Instead, they emphasize aquaculture. That is, they believe that we must plant gardens and cultivate farms in the sea—and observe good crop management, just as we should have been doing on land these many centuries. If we continue to behave recklessly with the world's resources and neglect to plan for the future, these folks say, we will not only destroy ourselves and the whales, but also a significant source of food for both!

Vegetable aquaculture is an accepted and familiar concept; it is already commonplace in science fiction literature. It takes a moment to realize, therefore, that fish culture is usually referred to only obliquely. It doesn't seem possible that we could isolate schools—or herds—of fish behind underwater fences and breed them as ranchers do cattle to keep the beef market going. Canadian nature writer Farley Mowat put the problem to be faced in stark but beautiful prose in his *A Whale for the Killing*, when he wrote of herring. The old-timers of Newfoundland told him how plentiful herring once were—there had been more than enough to give the east coast of Canada an industry to feed people and the fin whales of that same coast a plentiful diet. In his short residence in a remote town on the Newfoundland coast, Mowat began to comprehend how overfishing had resulted in the virtual disappearance of the herring, a staple in both human and cetacean diet.

At this point, many human beings can still buy fish from markets of other parts of the world and put off their starvation for a while, but what can the whales do? Inevitably they will starve, like the human populations in places such as Bangladesh or parts of India, where people starve to death because they cannot go out and simply buy food.

Some day the portion of the human population which can now afford to buy, say, herring from another part of the world will run out of luck; the oceans will run out of herring everywhere. This is the rationale behind Iceland's "cod war," and the reason why nations are increasing their efforts to extend their national boundaries, within which other nations cannot fish to two hundred miles from shore. The growing competition for food is also the motivation behind Ecuador's "tuna war" against the United States. It explains Japan's and Russia's billion-dollar investments in pelagic (open-sea) fishing fleets which are self-sustaining for months at a time. These fleets leave the crew free to fish, even to can fish, while they are thousands of miles from home port—in other nations' fishing grounds. These countries have simply fished out their own fisheries.

It is still difficult to imagine the day when all the fish will have been taken from the sea before they have had a chance to reproduce and mature. It may be impossible for some to envision the day when the land mass is so completely overpopulated room enough to grow food will no longer exist. Yet many of us are old enough to remember the orange groves of Southern California which have now been replaced by endless subdivisions. Is the earth being swallowed up by sheer numbers of people and the dwellings which house them?

Overfishing—uncontrolled—is impoverishing the world of the whale. When we think of the real reasons behind the tuna wars and the cod wars; of the sudden disappearance of sardines which once fed Monterey's Cannery Row with a seemingly endless supply; of the agricultural lands which turned into dust basins, perhaps we can just begin to imagine a day when the earth will no longer feed the animals of the earth, nor the seas feed the whales and the fishes.

We know that stocks of herring which fed the finners in some parts of the world have been overfished and are gone for good. But do you know what's happening right now? Japanese whalers, foremost among those exhausting the world's whale population, have now started to go after krill, the main food of the humpbacks and grays. It seems they have decided that the day is coming when there will be so few whales that going after the remainders will be unprofitable. Therefore, they must find other prey to pay off the costs of the fleet. Their solution: Let's eat what the whales eat! And so krill cakes and krill meal, similar to fish cakes and fish meal, have already been introduced to Japanese consumers—with apparent success, according to the reports.

The message I get out of these frightening developments is simple: The fate of the human race and the fate of the whales are one and the same. We ought to get together! People who believe that the life cycle is never-ending are not very far-sighted with regard to life-sustaining resources. When the food is gone the life cycle on our planet will end too.

It's that simple.

*Returning to Lahaina at moonrise
after a day of whalewatching aboard the squarerigger* Rendezvous.

5

Whalewatching off Maui

F ew youngsters have had as exciting an introduction to the whales as my friend Michael Schoepp, to whom this book is dedicated. It took place in February, 1975, when he was thirteen. About forty members of what was soon to be organized as the Maui Chapter of the American Cetacean Society, including chapter president Charles B. Sutherland of Lahaina, had chartered the romantic old square-rigged brigantine *Rendezvous* for a Sunday's whalewatching in the Lahaina Roadstead. Mike and I were among the passengers, a group of island residents and winter visitors who more or less knew each other. It was a rather slow day for whalewatching, but the *Rendezvous*, a regular member of the Lahaina charter fleet, is a unique boat which manages to combine beauty with great seaworthiness. A fair breeze, and she sailed well; a strong breeze, and she sailed magnificently.

And in a flat calm, she sailed not at all. It was toward noon, and we had made only one or two distant sightings. We had seen blows, but none of the humpbacks had come close. As the sun rose higher in the sky, the heat increased. The engine was not running, and *Rendezvous* was almost dead in the water, somewhat closer to Lanai than to Maui in an area where the channel between the islands is about nine miles wide. One of the whalewatchers decided that it would be a good time for a swim. He stood poised on the rail for a moment, and then dived in. This looked like a good idea to the younger set—Lahaina kids rarely wear more than a swim suit and a T-shirt—and within seconds the deck looked like a football playing field after an especially flagrant foul: T-shirts flew in swarms like towels. Kids yelped and jumped overboard.

After a few minutes the swimmers were all refreshed. A few who were only winter residents of Maui suddenly looked into the water, as the sun shafted downward into what looked like an endless spiral, and became a little nervous; the sun's rays under such circumstances exaggerate the sense of depth. Some started to crawl back on board.

Suddenly there was a tremendous upheaval of water and a sound I recognized instantly—a sound similar to the deep roar of steam escaping under tremendous pressure. I looked around just in time to see the humpback's head still above water as he inhaled; then he sounded again. All this took place within twenty feet of the swimmers.

Those in the water were panic-stricken. Their faces were grim and the water was filled with the furious churning of arms and legs as they raced to the rope ladder on the side of the *Rendezvous*. I watched Mike closely; perhaps he saw that my face registered no alarm at all. He suddenly stopped swimming and trod water for a moment. The panic left his face. It was replaced by an expression of surprise, then with a wonderful smile of discovery. He turned away from the *Rendezvous* and looked toward the spot where the whale had first appeared. He then turned around and asked me, "Where'd it go?" I replied, "Under the boat. We'll probably see him on the other side in a couple of minutes."

Mike swam around the aft of the *Rendezvous* and watched. Sure enough, some two hundred yards distant, the humpback surfaced. He appeared to take three or four leisurely inhales as he swam forward, then he sounded from view.

Mike swam around and climbed back up on deck. He didn't say anything, but his grin spoke volumes. Mike had met his first humpback, and he'd been an allright guy!

As I mentioned earlier, I began my own whalewatching career, during the 1974-75 season, from atop Captain Les West's *Coral See*. The *Coral See* is, of course, a power-driven boat. Whalewatchers used to think that a silent sailboat was the best craft for whalewatching, but eventually this proved not to be true. A skipper aboard a powerboat who knows his business and understands whales actually appears to have the advantage. The early misinformation stemmed partly from conjecture generated, again, by the general lack of solid information about whales; and partly because much of the early whalewatching activity in Lahaina took place on the *Coral See*. The skippers of excursion boats do have an obligation to get in some coral gazing, despite the lack of complaints when whales are substituted for coral. The *Coral See's* schedule did have to be taken into consideration. It made three cruises a

Two whales of a pod of six. They circled the Rendezvous *in pairs.*

day, and some of them were timed to within a few minutes of a tourist bus's departure. This left little flexibility in the ninety-minute water excursion. There was just no time to go after whales more than a mile or so from shore. Nevertheless, we did manage to see a lot of whales in those early days—enough to get me hooked on whalewatching forever.

Captain West understood the whales. He soon developed a technique for whalewatching which was remarkably similar to one later recommended by the National Marine Fisheries Service of the Department of Commerce, the agency charged with executing the intent of the Marine Mammals Protection Act. He would head toward a pod, then slacken off and run parallel with the whales at the whales' own speed. If the animals appeared to be in a playful mood, he would idle the engines so that the *Coral See* moved only as dictated by the whim of wind or current. During these periods the whales often came up to us. If, however, the engine were shut off, or if the boat's speed were changed suddenly, the whales would usually disappear, apparently frightened by the uneven change of pitch or by the sudden silence.

The *Rendezvous* came onto the scene during the 1975 season, and then the observers who were trying to out-think the whales came up with the idea that a silent sailing boat was necessary for a successful whalewatching cruise. An informal group of us chartered the *Rendezvous*, some ninety feet of beautiful sailboat, three times that season, and we sighted whales three times as well. Once the activity we saw was spectacular; the other two times it was only so-so.

In all three cases, the hull of the *Rendezvous* did appear to arouse the curiosity of the whales. There was that first instance, when Mike unexpectedly found himself swimming with the curious whale who had come up to see what was going on. During the greatest of all the *Rendezvous* cruises, a pod of six whales played around us for an hour and twenty minutes. They arrived as a single pod, then broke up into pairs. By twos they circled the boat, close in or at a distance of perhaps 150 yards at the most. Or they remained under water, then surfaced in pairs with that thunderous hiss, as close as 15 feet from our hull. Sometimes they would surface aft, sometimes forward under the long bowsprit, sometimes directly abeam. And sometimes they would sound on one side, swim directly under the boat, and surface on the other side. After a while, three or four of those aboard decided to jump in with the whales. They reported that a porpoise was often leading one of the pairs in the underwater romps. I never did see the porpoise surface, although he obviously had to.

In the 1976 season we used yet a third boat, a classic 1929 Stephens motor yacht, the *Vida Mia*, which usually went on daily excursions to Manele Bay, Lanai, to take tourists on a beach picnic. On weekends, owner Chuck Clark decided to run it on whalewatching cruises on a first-come first-served basis. He did so at my suggestion. I continued to look for ways to get closer to the humpbacks and to photograph them. In return for his cooperation, I helped publicize the whalewatching cruises. I set an arbitrary limit of thirty persons per trip because it is difficult to take pictures with more aboard; someone's head is always popping thoughtlessly in front of the lens during the excitement of contact with the humpbacks. Once again, what I felt had been proved in the *Coral See* was confirmed by Clark's yacht, the *Vida Mia*. With an intelligent skipper at the controls, the sound of the engine did not frighten away the whales. My best contacts with the whales and my best pictures of the 1976 season were taken from aboard the *Vida Mia*.

I had started the season in December, 1975, aboard the *Coral See* and aboard the power yacht of a friend, Phil Cole. His *Hood* is a forty-foot cruiser. I had made some early-season humpback sightings from both vessels in which we were close enough to photograph the whales. Later, I started making the Lanai runs aboard *Vida Mia* whenever I had a day free. And when the season really started toward the end of January —that is, when the migrating whales had accumulated in Hawaiian waters in sufficient numbers to make expensive efforts worthwhile—I organized whalewatching cruises aboard the *Vida Mia* and *Rendezvous* on Saturdays and Sundays in the hopes of preventing possible harassment to the whales by keeping an eye on the commercial activity. For two solid months, both boats were booked to capacity every weekend, and usually by different people. Repeats were from a few hardcore whalewatchers such as myself. Tourists visiting Maui for three or four days learned of the unadvertised $10-per-person, bring-your-own-lunch cruises, and there were only slightly fewer of them than there were members of what we on Maui call the "condominium set"—those who own a condo unit and stay for three to five months of each year. It was among the latter group that the majority of the repeaters were found. Once in a while, a tourist would go out two days in a row, and occasionally one would extend a stay to cover two weekends.

The 1976 *Rendezvous* cruises produced a number of good sightings, and as usual, even the one-cruise tourists, especially those from inland America, were thrilled by the briefest glimpse of the whales. Some of these people, when treated to their first close view of a humpback, spontaneously burst into applause!

Patterns in whalewatching emerged. On some days the whales seemed more skittish than others. It appears that a lone whale is much less curious, much less venturesome, and much more cautious than a whale in a pod. Like people, whales take courage in numbers. We had our greatest experiences when we came upon pods. Some days they all appeared to be traveling from one island to another—say, from Maalaea Bay at Central Maui, north to Molokai. Then they would be scarce, from a whalewatching point of view, for several days. Most of the time, the pods appeared to follow a giant circular path which could be traced within an area that can be seen almost entirely from Lahaina. This area includes Maalaea and the eastern tip of Kahoolawe at the southern end, the Kaanapali-Napili region north of Lahaina, and, at the other end, Lanai, across the channel.

T hose of us who watch for the annual return of the whales start scanning the waters between Lahaina and Lanai as early as November. While the whales are found off Kauai and the Big Island to some extent, Hawaii's most frequent sightings take place within the circle just described. The Lahaina Roadstead is Hawaii's traditional whalewatching ground; this common knowledge was verified by an inconclusive whale census undertaken in 1976. I say "inconclusive" because those who directed it felt that a fair picture would be obtained over a period of three different weekends, but in actuality the whale count was made on only two weekends. The third was cancelled because of high sea conditions. With white caps and flying spray, it is difficult to spot whales in the water, or to tell spouts from spindrift. In charge of the census, which he called the Whale Blitz, was Dr. Edward W. Shallenberger, vice president and director of operations for Oahu's Sea Life Park. (The term "blitz" was used, he said, because they were "hitting them from all sides at once"—that is, the whale count employed observers on land, sea, and in the air all at the same time.) Working with Shallenberger was Rick Gaffney, then the Sea Grant representative on Maui (Sea Grant is a Federally-funded program for ocean resource study and development), whalewatcher president Chuck Sutherland, and Jim Hudnall.

Because Shallenberger, from a scientist's point of view, did not feel that two weekends of observations were conclusive, he speaks in his report only of tentative findings. Still, the Whale Blitz indicated a total Hawaii humpback population of around two hundred. The majority of the sightings were in the waters between West Maui and Lanai, and between Molokai and Lanai.

The most common whale sightings are made from land, and those in the Lahaina area are usually made in the late afternoon. This is because the sun is then shining toward Lahaina, illuminating from behind the blows sent up by the surfacing whales and making these blows stand out sharply against the purple background of Lanai. This lighting pattern is one of the factors contributing to Lahaina's reputation as a whalewatching center. The humpbacks travel closer to Lanai than to Maui late in the afternoon—possibly when the plankton starts to rise toward the surface again. At this time the humpbacks' characteristically bulb-shaped blows seem to dot the horizon against Lanai. Observers from the shore can also see, from time to time, flashes of light as the sun gleams off the great surfacing bodies.

Because of the volcanic nature of the Hawaiian Islands, great numbers of what we call lava tubes exist throughout the region. These are just what the name implies: old, inactive tubes—giant hoses, if you will—ascending from what was once a source of lava upwards to the surface. Small lava lakes beneath the surface of the earth's crust were exhausted, drained, and in other ways emptied out through these natural aqueducts, and now only the holes and tunnels to the surface remain. Up in the mountains rain is caught in these underground reservoirs, and we benefit from them as a major source of water. Just because the ancient lava flow may have been located in an area now under water does not mean that the flow of fresh water downward from the mountain reservoirs has been halted. Sailors know that the seas between the islands are dotted with fresh-water pockets. Experienced seamen such as Captain West can spot them visually. He tells me that the humpbacks like to swim through them. He thinks that the fresh water not only refreshes the whales, but that it also has something to do with a phenomenon which is just beginning to attract scientific attention: The humpbacks appear to shed many of their parasitic barnacles while in the waters of Hawaii, and no one really knows why this is so.

I mentioned Captain West's hypothesis to Paul J. Struhsaker when he spoke to the Maui whalewatchers early in 1976. Struhsaker is the supervising fishery biologist at the Honolulu office of the National Marine Fisheries Service. West's observation was especially interesting to him because the project he was then involved in was attempting to learn why the humpbacks lose their barnacles while in Maui waters. He did not believe that the fresh water killed or weakened the barnacles, but he did think that the change from Arctic to Hawaii waters had much to do with the phenomenon.

He told us that this hypothesis took form after he had communicated with a friend, a commercial shrimp trawler who worked in the Pailolo Channel between Maui and Molokai.

The friend, Struhsaker said, came to him and said, "Eh! I started getting these barnacles last January when the humpback whales started showing up." The shrimper handed him eight or ten long barnacles which he had picked up in his nets. And, Struhsaker told his whale-watcher audience, "He put forth the idea that the whales are actually dropping the barnacles when they are here in the Islands." The barnacles which were handed to him were a species known to live only on baleen whales, "and the logical host for this specimen would be Megaptera (humpback), of course."

Struhsaker wondered if the tropical or subtropical waters had some effect on the barnacle or the skin of the humpbacks, either making the barnacles drop off or loosening them so that the whale can easily remove them by scraping his body against the ocean floor in Hawaii's shallower waters.

He said the matter needed considerable study, and that it had received almost no scientific attention at all. Some lay references to the phenomenon did exist though. One, dated from 1910, when Norwegian whalers working southwest of Africa reportedly saw whales "arrive heavily infested (with barnacles) and leave either clean or with juvenile (barnacles)." And the British Antarctic Expedition of the early 1900s reported that it was "common knowledge" among the New Zealand whalers that whales "actively remove barnacles during their inshore movements off the bottom. . . . Similar behavior has been reported off Oahu, and in black coral beds and off Bermuda," Struhsaker told us. "Do warmer waters have an influence on the physiological condition of the skin so that the barnacle might be more easily removed?" he wondered.

Folklore and common experience often come up with the same answers that careful, drawn-out scientific investigations do. Frequently, in reply to talk of some scientifically predictable sea or weather phenomenon an old salt will say, "I could have told you that." That's the difference between scientific minds, which must catalogue everything carefully and study findings before coming to a conclusion, and laypeople who know things because it has been their experience that such and such is so.

I therefore mentioned Struhsaker's talk to Captain David Russell, referred to earlier in these pages. His reply to the observation that humpbacks lose barnacles in warm Hawaiian waters? "I could have told you that."

Any sailor who has worked aboard a wooden boat, no matter how small, has seen water changes cause barnacles to drop off the hull, Russell said. Traveling up the Sacramento River from the San Francisco Bay produces this effect, in this case probably because the change from salt to fresh water kills the barnacle. Russell pointed out that over the centuries sailors have noted that changing seas—that is, going from one of the world's oceans to another—also causes barnacles to drop off. The only problem is, however, that while barnacles from one part of the world will drop off a boat's hull—and presumably a whale's body—those native to the waters the ship is currently plying will grow on in their place!

A number of eyewitnesses have reported to me that they have seen whales here in Hawaii so close to land that they appeared to be stranded. These reports have come from both Oahu and Maui, and especially Maui's Kihei area. The witness generally describes the whale as furiously floundering about in an apparent effort to escape. Later, by some miracle usually attributed to an unusual rise in tide, the whale departs. Actually, those who have watched the whales over a period of years feel that these "stranded" whales are just "scratching their backs"—knocking off the weakened barnacles. I believe this explanation also applies to much of the leaping activity which so many writers call "frolicking" and point to as proof of the humpback's "playful nature."

I do think the humpback is playful, however. From repeated observation, I conclude that all marine mammals share this trait. These animals are too intelligent to simply pass the day by eating, swimming, and making love. The little whales not only enjoy the games they learn as performers at the seaquariums, but they are also capable, according to Lilly, of making up their own games. However, as my photographs show, humpbacks leap up into the air and come back down on their backs repeatedly. One series of photos I took of the same whale engaged in this activity made more than fifty successive, leisurely leaps. I went through two twenty-exposure rolls of color film and one of black and white, and each change of film required a couple minutes while this whale leapt in and out of the sea. Was there a hidden purpose to this behavior?

Some believe this activity to be a form of communication; they think that the whale makes these resounding whacks on the water to attract the attention of a whale some distance away. I can't agree with this theory. The humpback's voice can be heard at least as far as the thwacking of the sea, and a whale version of, "Halloo, where are you?" would be easier and more effective in locating fellow whales than beating the waters. At the time I was watching this particular leaping activity, I strongly felt the humpback was having a good time—and that contributing to the good time was a satisfying scratch of the barnacle itch.

The humpbacks also "lobtail"—the term refers to a whacking of the flukes against the waters, causing a loud sound and a frothy sea. I believe whales lobtail for one of two reasons, if not for both: to get the barnacles off the flukes—and I have seen these little crustaceans on the top and edges of the flukes in large numbers—or to attract attention. Any time I have seen humpbacks lobtail, at least one other humpback has been nearby, sometimes within reach. Therefore, this attention-getting technique could even be a form of courtship. Some observers think that the leaping behavior is a form of courtship as well, but I do not. What good would it do to thrash around when no other whale was in sight?

A humpback as he "lobtails"—whacks the water with his flukes.

One reward for persistent whalewatching is that it becomes possible after a while to distinguish one whale from another and to identify old friends. One distinctive feature of the humpback is skin-color pattern. White skin appears not only on the underside from the chin down, but also on the underside of the flukes and flippers. In some instances, the white goes over to the top of the flippers as well, but I have never known of a case where it was also atop the tailflukes. The white pattern of the humpback is inconsistent from whale to whale and, as nearly as I can determine, never exactly the same.

In one of his 1975 talks to Maui's whalewatchers, Jim Hudnall suggested that the dorsal fin could also serve as a means of distinguishing individuals. He said that the dorsal fin comes in such a variety of shapes and sizes that it can be used to tell one individual humpback from another. My repeated observations of this distinction tend to confirm the theory. Photographs I have seen also show that the fin shape in a mother whale is often inherited by her offspring. Thus, fin shape together with individual white markings and the sometimes very minor differences in the shape of the flukes appear to suggest that humpbacks have individual characteristics just as people do.

This theory is not new. Both Hudnall's and my own observations reinforce an earlier statement made by Paul Budker: "I cannot remember ever seeing two humpbacks with the same coloration. . . . [H]umpbacks are evidently individualists as regards the wearing of uniform." He wrote that in 1959.

Photographs taken of a number of whales bear out the differences. Hudnall cautiously claims that he can identify the same whales in photographs taken in two separate years. My photographs in this book show some humpbacks more than once, and at different locations off Maui. They also show that the white markings are not uniform, although I cannot identify any one whale in these photographs solely on the basis of white markings. The photos of the whale leaping out of the water (p. 99), and the photo of the whale spyhopping (p. 101; an activity to be described shortly) were taken on two separate days. I'm sure that these pictures are of the same whale, though not enough of the body shows to prove such a statement. This unprovable feeling goes back to an earlier reference to my belief in a mystical rapport between human beings and whales. Somehow I *know* these whales are one and the same. But science doesn't accept hunches!

A humpback leaping completely out of the water.

W|hether it was from *Vida Mia* or the *Rendezvous*, each whalewatch-ing trip seemed to add a new dimension to either the knowledge or interest of Maui's devoted whalewatchers. The humpbacks and the world they lived in were always fresh, and each new encounter somehow had some of the excitement of that very first close contact. Though many people remained content with viewing the silver puffs against the Lanai horizon, the numbers of those who took to the water in boats for a closer view increased season by season. The whalewatcher traffic in the 1976 season was truly astounding. A comment made by Mary Rodriguez, a writer from Monterey, California, who spends a month to six weeks on Maui every year, summed up the psychology behind the trend: "Every time someone saw a spout, I'd turn around and look," she told me. "I'd spend hours looking out my window, trying to catch a glimpse of them, usually just the blow. But after that day aboard the *Vida Mia* and being almost able to touch them, I no longer get a thrill out of seeing them from land. I guess I'm spoiled, but I've got to be out there with them now!" On Mary's first day aboard *Vida Mia* a humpback leaped into the air very close to us. No wonder she has become a bit blasé about observing from the shore!

The world of the whale is rarely the same. The first close sighting I had in the 1976 season was in December, 1975, when I made a day-long cruise aboard Phil Cole's motor yacht, *Hood*. He had a couple of people on board for a sportfishing charter, and I tagged along in hopes of seeing the first whale of the season. It was not a good day for whalewatching; it was quite windy and the sea was kicking up whitecaps in several areas. We trolled all the way to Lanai and along the relatively protected south coast of that island. Then we "went around the corner," as the sailors say, back into the wind. The sea was very choppy and the fishermen were having no luck. Phil steered quite close in to those high, dark-brown, sheer cliffs which have been formed by the land simply breaking off and falling into the sea. I was topside on the flying bridge and was concentrating on the water. I had about given up hopes for a sighting and had set aside my camera when I suddenly became aware of some-thing strange—an eye was looking at me from the water. That's all my first impression was: one big eye, boring right into me. The moment it disappeared again beneath the waves I came to. I reached for my camera, and at the same time I had a mental image of what was there besides the

A "spyhopping" humpback.

eye. I was sure I was right. It was a large, bulb-shaped head; and when it went down, I could see a back, but ever so fleetingly. It had been a pilot whale. My impression was that it was about twenty feet long at the most.

I told Phil, and he said that pilot whales had been spotted quite frequently in this area for the past two weeks. He repeated a common theory, which may be only popular fiction, that the pilot whales are just that—pilots, or advance guards for the big whales.

The pilot whale I had seen was doing what is known as "spyhopping." He had been in a vertical position, "treading water" as it were, and keeping his eye above the surface of the water so he could see what was going on. All cetaceans apparently do this, although not until later in the same season did I first see a humpback spyhop. Needless to say, because of the size of the humpback, it was a much more spectacular sight. The pilot whale, also called the blackfish in some parts of the world, has some white markings on the underside of its body which, unlike the white on the humpback, has a clearly delineated pattern. However, the pilot's markings are not as extensive as those of the orca. In fact, this pilot did not come out of the water far enough for me to see the white.

I will never forget that first impression, though; the eye was looking straight at me so forcefully that I could see nothing else for a moment. And somehow, it had managed to convey to me the impression that the pilot whale didn't appreciate in the least that I was there for the sole purpose of spying on him!

About a half-hour later I made my first humpback sighting of the season. Just previous to it I had a familiar feeling which I cannot rationally explain. Nevertheless, it is a feeling I had developed during earlier years of whalewatching: I was aware of the presence of humpbacks before I actually saw them. Only a second or two elapsed between awareness and contact; after another few seconds the humpbacks had breathed and headed back under again. As I saw them, I automatically snapped my camera's shutter, and the resulting picture shows all I saw that day of the humpbacks: One had his magnificent back arched in an attitude of sounding, head and flukes underwater; the other directly in front of the first had started to sound a split second earlier and already had head and back submerged—flukes in the air, poised against his buddy's arching back. In this one picture, (see p. 103), the "wheel" motion previously described as the origin of the word "whale" is clearly demonstrated.

This photo shows two stages of the "wheeling" motion, the origin of the word "whale."

Later in the season, the seas were quite often more peaceful. On one excursion, this time aboard the *Sport Diver*, which young Tad Luckey charters mostly to scuba divers or sportfishermen, we again returned to the waters off Lanai's south side. As we approached Manele Bay I noticed a frothing fury of motion close in toward the cliffs. I asked Tad what was going on, and he headed over toward the commotion. It turned out to be the large school of dolphins which had been sighted recently with regularity in the region. As we approached them, they turned as a group—more than a hundred of them—and headed toward us. The speed these little whales are capable of always amazes me. They appear to gather speed for the sheer joy of it. On this occasion, the main school headed toward us and then eventually divided, the majority of them swimming on one side, to pass by us. Then, with a great flurry which evoked in my imagination a rather cartoonlike vision of the little guys sticking their flukes forward like brakes and skidding to a stop, they reversed direction and swam in a semicircle around us. They then gathered speed and darted by us again. A few individuals seemed to come to a complete stop, then pour on the speed and shoot past us in an obvious display of their abilities. The mouths of dolphins are formed in a perpetual grin, but even taking that into account, the speeding individuals seemed pleased with themselves.

Some dolphins broke off from the main group and performed the trick for which they have been famous since early times: They skim along and playfully leap back and forth alongside the boat and then in front of the bow in an obvious game of "sea chicken." Naturally, they never get hit!

Speed? While the dolphins were thus frolicking I used up an entire twenty-exposure roll of film. I got a lot of splashes for my trouble, but only once did I manage to catch some heads out of the water clearly enough to show that these were bottlenose dolphins—the kind most commonly seen in the seaquariums. During a similar incident, also from the *Hood*, the same thing happened: Out of twenty shots, only one picture showed the dolphins clearly enough so that they could be identified as spinner dolphins. The spinner, by the way, gets its popular name from its habit of leaping into the air and spinning around at the same time. I would estimate that these dolphins leap as high as twelve to fifteen feet above the surface of the water in some of their jumps. It is both impressive and amusing to see a herd of them doing this, with perhaps half a dozen out of a group of forty or fifty leaping and spinning at the same time. I know of no explanation for their behavior, except that they leap and spin for the fun of it.

In *Whales and Dolphins*, Slijper says that dolphins can swim in short bursts in excess of 20 knots. The visual impression they make during these sessions when they go shooting past the boat is that they travel much faster.

When the dolphins are swimming at a more leisurely pace, their blows can be seen just as the whales' can. When they are near a boat, they rarely dive very deep. They are mainly creatures of the near-surface anyway, and if they breathe two or three times a minute, they could easily do so without making special trips to the air. At the same time, they appear to "hold" their breath for only two or three minutes at a stretch, and the mist of their blows looks more like a dying drinking fountain than anything else. They always seem to be pushing some water out of the way as they skim along right at the surface, and the blow is sometimes lost from sight in the splashing of their movement forward. When it is visible, it is but a tiny puff which dissipates almost immediately.

Dolphins often swim with the whales—not in large numbers, but singly or in twos or fours. Just as we started one cruise in late February, 1976, I thought I spotted such a partnership. We had hardly nosed out of Lahaina's harbor aboard the *Vida Mia* when I saw an adult whale swimming, almost floating, very slowly in the flat-calm water. Beside it was a small bump in the water from which little blows—more bubbles than blows, really—came intermittently. We slowly edged our way toward the pair, then slacked off and took the prescribed parallel course, moving at the animals' speed. The smaller bump turned out to be a days-old humpback.

The sound of our engine was obviously of concern to the mother, but she would neither speed up nor sound. The baby was just learning how to conduct the breathing-diving cycle. In the first few weeks of life, baby whales can go no more than three to five minutes without surfacing for air.

A days-old humpback and his mother.

Note that the calf is now to the right of the adult.
The mother put herself between us and the calf as we approached on the Vida Mia.

To solve the problem of our encroachment without sounding, the mother altered course slowly, widening the angle between the *Vida Mia* and herself and her baby and always staying between us and the baby. The first time we approached them, we were on the side of the mother. We followed them for about twenty minutes, at their own slow pace and always parallel, then went away in order not to upset the mother too much. About an hour later we spotted what turned out to be the same pair again. At first, we saw only the mother, and we headed for her. Then we saw the baby between her body and our boat. The mother immediately put herself between us and her calf, but never once did she show panic or pick up speed. We didn't tarry long, for we all felt that they had suffered their share of scrutiny for one day. I was particularly concerned that we might be interfering with the baby's feeding cycle and requested that the skipper change course and look for other whales instead. My photographs show exactly all that we saw of mother and child—varying degrees of exposure of the area fore and aft of the blow hole. The water around them rippled very little even in the calmest seas, for their progress was slow, absolutely steady, and even in their attempt to widen the gap between us they did not rush or panic.

Sometimes whalewatchers get the distinct feeling not that they are encroaching on family relations, but that the animals they seek out recognize their good will and actually turn to them for help. In such cases information has to be conveyed from whale to human, and because the two species speak different languages, "conversation" has to be carried out in what amounts to sign language—the alternative that two people will resort to if neither speaks the other's language.

A particularly dramatic example of such interaction involved the Eldon Coon family, formerly of Alaska and now of Lahaina, who conduct all-day excursions for tourists from Lahaina to Lanai aboard their two trimarans, *Trilogy* and *White Bird*. It happened early in March, 1976. At midafternoon on the day at hand, Randy, one of the two Coon sons, was in charge of *White Bird*. Shortly after the boat departed Lanai, a great humpback whale surfaced in front of it. *White Bird* had not yet accumulated much speed. Crew and passengers alike were fascinated as the humpback surfaced close to the boat and then approached even closer.

She came toward *White Bird* head on, slowly but deliberately. By this time the trimaran was almost motionless in the water. The humpback advanced slowly but purposefully up to one of the trimaran's hulls, and ever so lightly bumped her head against it. Then she backed off, without sounding. She looked up on deck and, as Randy reported it, "we all knew she was trying to tell us something," though at first no one could imagine what the message might be. The whale repeated the head-bumping three or four times, each time backing off and directing her giant head upward to look at those on deck.

Randy finally got the idea that something was wrong. He donned a face mask and snorkel and dived into the water near the whale. Once beneath the surface, he saw that she did indeed have trouble: She had started to give birth, but something had gone wrong and the baby was caught half-in and half-out. Further, by whale standards the birth was breech; that is, the calf was coming out head-first. In a normal whale birth, the calf comes out tail-first, presumably so that it is headed right toward the surface after becoming free of the mother's body. The baby's first breaths must be above water, of course, as with any other air-breathing animal. If it breathed during any stage of birth while still under water it would drown.

The whale mother often appears to have the assistance of a "midwife" or "auntie" while she is giving birth. The midwife has been observed to push the baby up to the surface of the water the instant it is free of the mother's body. Dr. Edward Shallenberger believes that the assistance of these second females at the time of birth, however, is generally over-rated. He feels that the mother usually gives birth unassisted, and that the second female is merely "company," or perhaps may have some sort of a protective role. Shallenberger thus holds that it is inaccurate to call this second female a "midwife."

Once the baby is born and breathing air the mother snaps the umbilical cord, usually by turning a giant somersault in the air. Actor Richard Demming, a resident of Kihei, Maui, and most recently remembered for his continuing role as governor of Hawaii in the *Hawaii 5-0* TV series, says he has witnessed this act. An ardent whalewatcher, he often goes out in his Hobie catamaran for a close look at the humpbacks. He told me in January, 1976, that two or three years ago, he had been out on his Hobie when he came across a mother whale with a calf so young that the cord was still attached. He said she had to leap out of the water several times before it snapped.

The mother whale who stopped the *White Bird* to ask for help, however, was in much more serious trouble. Randy said that she was silent but obviously pleading. The baby appeared to have been stuck for some time. In the distance, he said, lurked a twelve-foot tiger shark. Reluctantly, realizing that he could do nothing to help, he climbed back on the *White Bird* and left.

I have never been able to document the details of what happened next, but I did learn that help came to the distressed whale. The reticence of the heroes to proclaim themselves was probably due to the provision of the Marine Mammal Protection Act which prohibits individuals from attempting to assist a marine mammal in either real or apparent distress. Instead, "official" help, such as a member of the Department of Fish and Game, must be summoned. In this case, by the time official help could have arrived from the island of Oahu, it would have been too late. Thus, we have an unsung hero or two in this incident; I suspect residents of both Lanai and Lahaina were involved. Whoever they were, some divers were able to lasso the by then dead infant and free it from the mother so she was out of danger and able to carry on. The act apparently took place one or two days after Randy's sighting aboard *White Bird.*

While still on the subject of birth, I would like to digress here briefly to resolve a local controversy. Three miles north of Lahaina is the Kaanapali hotel resort area where most Maui tourists stay. Within the resort area is a shopping complex called Whalers Village. It is a series of tourist-oriented shops, galleries, and restaurants of quite high quality. A series of exhibits, for the most part in outdoor glass display cases, is devoted to whales and whaling. While the exhibits obviously have the commercial purpose of leading visitors, step by step, throughout the entire shopping complex, they are not cheap gimmicks. The displays are originals, often costly and relatively rare, and worthy of the "museum" designation they bear. The complex is a popular destination for school class outings.

However, at the entrance to the complex is a rather unfortunate statue. Its image is used in a number of ways by those connected with Whalers

Village—on stationery, in advertising, and so forth. This logo is unfortunate because it gives the false impression that twin births among whales is a common thing. It shows a mother humpback suckling two babies. As we shall see, twin births are not impossible, but they are extremely uncommon among cetaceans.

In 1974 and 1975, the first trained whalewatchers started coming to Maui in significant numbers and with increasing regularity. Some of these visitors immediately pounced upon this aesthetically pleasing, if scientifically misleading, bit of statuary; it briefly became fashionable to sneer at it. But I have long believed that every myth has its roots in truth. I set out to learn why this logo showed a mother whale with twins, when it appeared that as a general rule twin births did not occur. Chuck Sutherland, president of the Maui Chapter of the American Cetacean Society, handed me the answer. It was contained in *The Marine Mammals of the Northwestern Coast of North America*, by Captain Charles Scammon, the discoverer of the humpbacks' Baja breeding grounds. No one has ever accused Scammon of manufacturing his zoology, and in the book is a sketch by Scammon which clearly shows a mother humpback suckling twins. Because of the Captain's reputation as a well-respected zoologist, it must be assumed that his sketch was based on a live observation.

Paul Budker confirms the whales' twin-bearing capacity in more modern observations. While he joins many of the rest of us in lamenting that much of what we know today is learned from dead whales, he cites reports by scientists who accompanied whaling expeditions to study the cadavers about to be committed to the vats. Budker writes that humpbacks have a relatively high ratio of twin births, and that all whales apparently have the capability to produce twins. Twins, he wrote, have been found inside the bodies of humpbacks taken off both coasts of Africa—the Gabon in the South Atlantic and Madagascar in the Indian Ocean. Budker does cite a four-year period ending in 1951 when only one twin pregnancy was reported. In another year, which he does not specify though presumably it was sometime after World War II, ten pregnant females were killed and two of them carried twins. In the 1949 season off Madagascar (Malagasy) he says 32 pregnant females were taken and among them were two sets of twins.

I have never seen a whale, humpback or otherwise, accompanied by twins. Nor have I ever heard personally of an eyewitness account of cow whales being accompanied by twin babies. I should think that nature would make this phenomenon a rarity, since mother and midwife would really have to be "on their toes" to deliver two babies to the surface within the critically short time span available.

The Whalers Village logo is seen by hundreds of thousands of tourists every year. It is not as inaccurate a representation as some believe. But the uninformed tourist whose only contact with the world of the whale may take place during a once-in-a-lifetime visit to Maui could get the impression from the logo that twins are common. The tourist might even receive the subliminal message that whales are reproducing rapidly. The fate of the whale populations is so tenuous that I feel it necessary to clear up even this small confusion. All hope for the whales lies in the understanding and empathy of human beings.

I began to make brief notes on some of my excursions during the whalewatching season. On February 22, 1976, for instance, I noted that we first encountered two adults with a very young calf which "bubbled more than spouted." We left them and then saw two pods at once. One pod had four whales in it, the other had three. We headed for the four, because we had learned that the more whales there are together, the less they are prone to spook and take off. One of the adults, I noted, "had an interesting pink line going from the caudal fin back for about four feet." It did not appear to be a wound, although later in the season, two different whales were seen with fresh cuts—single slashes which appeared to have been made by the keel of a shallow-draft boat, such as a small speedboat. Could someone in a boat have been harrassing the whales? Such cuts look horribly painful, but all the cetaceans have proved to have remarkable regenerative powers and such wounds generally heal quickly.

Later the same day we came upon a group of spinner dolphins—apparently by mutual agreement. They swam about us as usual, often in their typical spying position: skimming past on their side, an eye looking up at us through the water. They ended up surfing on the wake of the *Vida Mia* for a few minutes until, apparently bored, they left us.

The wind had picked up, and we soon came upon a school of flying fish. We were treated to the sight of them leaping off one wave and remaining airborne for fifteen seconds or more before crashing into another. Their bodies and "wings" glistened in the sunlight because they are covered with a mucus-like oil which apparently facilitates their flights.

We made no further sightings for a couple hours. Then—according to my notes it was 3 P.M.—we came upon a pod of six humpbacks with one baby. A small herd of dolphins constantly played among the whales. We stayed with them for an hour and ten minutes. We hardly moved and the pod appeared to stay with us voluntarily. They seemed to verify the observation that the larger the group of whales, the less concerned they appear to be about the presence of humans.

The whales swam, sounded briefly, surfaced and breathed; they did so both as a group and in pairs. One adult and the baby remained rather aloof from the rest, and on the far side of the main pod from us. Once, one of the adult whales engaged in quick spyhopping activity, but he apparently dismissed us so quickly it was almost insulting. Toward the end of their romp, they picked up a little speed and headed north. We continued alongside them. Once they stopped again and engaged in some diving and surfacing, all within a small area and all within thirty or forty feet of the boat. They then took to diving and surfacing, again quickly, either beside us or on the opposite side of the boat. This lasted for some ten minutes, then they moved on again. It was not a forced move, but more like a bunch of kids coming home from school—kids who would have been tossing a ball back and forth as they progressed down their street to home. It's always easy to picture some human activity like that when watching whale activity.

As I watched the dolphins constantly intermingling with the whales during this romp, I realized that this companionship is quite usual, especially when a whale calf is present. I wondered if dolphins may at times form some sort of a protective alliance with mother whales. Dolphins in herds can knock out a shark in a hurry; an individual dolphin, despite the many romantic legends to the contrary, appears to have less than an even chance against an individual shark, however.

One of the most interesting experiences of the 1976 season was a series of sightings of a seven-whale pod. I first started seeing this pod early in February, and sighted it periodically until early May. The pod was seen every weekend but one, when I can only assume it

The humpbacks coming in close to the Vida Mia *in pairs.*

was off in the trench toward Molokai, perhaps on a feeding trip. The "Magnificent Seven" stuck together. The first time I saw them I was aboard the *Vida Mia*. They obviously noticed us, but the sound of the boat's engine did not evoke panic in them. Of course, we took precautions not to alarm them. Once we were in their vicinity, we throttled down to their speed, which was practically a drift rather than a forward motion. The captain tried to steer the *Vida Mia* on a parallel course with the pod, but this soon became impossible to hold. The humpbacks themselves drifted first to one side of us, then to the other, and at times they were on both sides of us.

They seemed more to ignore us than anything else. They were behaving naturally and most of all they just seemed to enjoy being whales! As my photographs show, they did nothing in unison, such as all sound at once, all surface at once, or anything else that indicated that our presence might be influencing them. Again, the larger the pod, the less concerned the whales seemed to be about human presence.

During this first sighting the whales sounded and showed flukes, generally reappearing within two or three minutes. Usually when we see flukes, it means the animals have gone down for a longer period of time, often with the purpose of putting some distance between the boat and themselves. But in this unconcerned activity pattern, they showed flukes in making quick, deep dives. They could have been diving either for the fun of it or to check out the food possibilities. But because they did nothing as a group, and repeated no motion with any regularity, it seems doubtful that their dives had any purpose other than enjoyment or variety. If the whales had been feeding, that is, if there had been something in the area to feed on, they would be more apt to do so as a pod.

Therefore, while one of two whales were sounding, others were surfacing, others were blowing, and still others were casually traveling on the surface. Simultaneously the pod was moving southward. They were making about two to three knots, as was the *Vida Mia*. At times a couple of the humpbacks—rarely one alone—would break away from the romping pod and come slowly toward the boat, effortlessly sound, and surface right alongside us. They would come up slightly listing to one side so that an eye could be cast toward us, but they were not so curious that they would assume a spyhopping position. Then, these mildly curious individuals would slowly glide by us in the direction opposite from ours, and two or three minutes later reappear up ahead with the main pod.

On this first sighting of the Magnificent Seven this casual activity went on for forty minutes. Then, without seeming at all alarmed the pod picked up speed and moved off. The whales would still occasionally show flukes and surface, and they still seemed to want to play; but they obviously had some destination in mind, and the time had come for them to get there. We did not follow them, partly because to do so would have been an obvious chase and therefore would have legally constituted harassment, and partly because they were headed south whereas we had to head back north to Lahaina.

The actions of the Magnificent Seven duplicated the patterns observed generally among the Maui-based humpbacks. All the whales in this area move from one place to another; they do not stay in a specific neighborhood. And they make their moves, usually, without too much hurry. They just seem to be under some compulsion, whether for food or for variety, to move about.

There is, however, a pattern to the day-to-day movements of Maui whales. Maalaea Bay—the indentation where West Maui and the rest of the island meet—appears to be the first destination of the expectant mothers as they arrive from the north. Jim Hudnall labeled this bay a "humpback nursery," because it is here that many of the babies are born. Thus, Maalaea Bay becomes something of a home port for the Maui humpbacks, and their travel patterns are best based from there.

From Maalaea they will travel north and pass Lahaina; then, they will turn west and visit either Molokai or Lanai. Finally, they skirt southward again by Kahoolawe, and end up in the Maalaea region once again. Sometimes a pod will take three or four days to complete this pattern—a swim of perhaps 75 miles.

We were discussing feeding patterns earlier. Every once in a while, during these Maui travels, a pod will break the pattern and go completely around the Island, where the water is deeper and small fish, such as those the tuna fishermen use for bait, are known to abound. I feel this indicates that the humpbacks do, indeed, eat fish occasionally while here. There is much more plankton continually available in the waters off Lanai, the waters that the whales normally cruise. The break in their cruise pattern indicates a break in the feeding pattern, not a search for variety of water itself.

The next time I saw the Magnificent Seven was as instructive as the first time. I somehow knew it was the same pod, yet I could count only five individuals. The five seemed more friendly and more attentive towards us than usual. They came up to the *Vida Mia*, whose engine was in idle, and seemed to make us their base of operations for the afternoon's games. They seemed to want to keep us in one place. One pair would swim by on one side of the boat, while another pair would swim by in the opposite direction on the other side. And one lone humpback repeatedly assumed the spyhop position. I went through several rolls of film with the one camera I had with me and photographed him spyhopping in both black and white and color. He spyhopped within twenty yards of the boat, and he did it for so long that he was either taking very careful looks at us or, less probably, he was attempting to attract our attention. If the latter was the case, he certainly succeeded!

On this particular afternoon, when the whales swam by us, either singly or in pairs, they came close in and swam in an unusual "tilting" position. That is, they surfaced and traveled slowly by us a little on one side so that they could keep an eye out of the water with which to look at us.

This went on for nearly an hour. I was alone atop the roof of *Vida Mia*, the ship's highest viewpoint. The whales' activity was so repetitive that after a while there was really nothing new to photograph. I settled back and tried to figure out what the whales were doing, and where the other two were. I was fascinated by their behavior; it seemed cool and calculated, and yet at the same time just a little sly. They were playing games with us and I knew it.

I noticed that when they went by us in one direction (north), they went a little farther past the boat than they did when passing us moving south. I started to put two and two together. Obviously, something besides us was interesting them, and whatever it was would be found in the direction they favored with longer swims.

I picked up my binoculars and scanned the waters to our immediate north. As I did so, one of the whales surfaced beside the *Vida Mia* with a louder snort than usual. I must conclude that this was a coincidence since I dare not imagine that the whale knew what I was doing and was trying to distract me. But I did find the answer to my question: Less than three hundred yards beyond us, swimming so slowly that they were hardly noticeable, were the other two whales of the pod—plus a brand new baby whale! The three were swimming in a rather wide circle. The baby was so young that both the mother and the auntie kept giving it encouraging little nudges to keep its head above water. Sometimes the baby would come part-way out of the water and lean against the mother, as if wanting to rest from the exertion of swimming, yet needing to take in fresh air. But it would quickly slide back into the water again.

I badly wanted to tell the rest of those aboard of my discovery, but I was sure that if I did, there would be no way to restrain human nature and prevent the skipper from steering the boat over toward the baby. The three were just a bit too far away to photograph well, and this was another reason I would like to have announced my sighting. Yet somehow I felt a silent pleading from the five who circled us closer and closer; and I was touched by the sight of the little whale calf, so young, so much in need of a few more hours to adapt to life outside the womb.

I continued to watch, fascinated both by what I saw and what I felt—extrasensory thought waves, if you will. Ten minutes later the skipper announced that it was time to head back for Lahaina, more than an hour away. Mentally I heaved a sigh of relief. The decision was no longer up to me! And once we were firmly committed to our new course, I announced my discovery. Everyone went aft for a quick glimpse, and I felt just a little smug.

I feel certain that the whale who continually spyhopped that afternoon was the baby's father, anxious that these strange creatures he did not quite understand should stay away from junior, mother, and auntie. That was on March 20, 1976. The Magnificent Seven, now eight, were seen for another month before they headed north, but usually as a pod of six. The mother and baby stuck together and stayed a little apart, although they did not stray too far from their basic family unit.

Q uite often while out whalewatching we would see a single blow, go over to the area, and wait for the whale to surface. When it did so it would usually be at some distance. Often what we thought was a single whale would turn out to be a pair. These whales would often be doing what is known as surface traveling. Whales that are surface traveling do not dive deep or stay below the surface very far. They are headed somewhere specific and they don't want to waste time descending and ascending. They will not even stop while taking in air. They

A surface traveling whale.

travel just below the surface, come up far enough to get their blow holes out of the water, and sink back into the water again. They look neither to right nor left. Whenever surface-traveling whales surfaced near our boat, they did not seem concerned or distracted. They had one thing in mind, travel, and that was all. I sighted surface-traveling whales much less frequently than frolicking, playing, and possibly feeding family units. The latter, of course, are clearly much more obvious to whalewatchers and invite their attention. The most striking thing about the traveling whales was their businesslike attitude. They knew what they wanted to do, and they were doing it—at six to twelve knots, at that! Such travelers are probably usually hurrying to rejoin their family unit.

Here in Hawaii the dramatically increasing interest in whales is especially noticeable in the Lahaina area. Lahaina had already developed a worldwide reputation as a port of call for whalers from about 1820 to 1871, the tourist industry continues to cultivate that reputation in its never-ending search for the tourist dollar. Part of the town's reputation as a still-functioning whaling center is legitimate. For instance, Lahaina is probably the best place in the Islands to find good scrimshaw. The making of scrimshaw—delicately etched pieces of whale ivory—is an original American folk art and it was practiced by many of the whalermen who came to Lahaina. Chuck Sutherland, already mentioned as president of the Maui Chapter of the American Cetacean Society, is a modern scrimshander. In his shop, The Whaler, he sells examples of the traditional nautical art. Sutherland has caught some flack from self-righteous crusaders who talk before they think, demanding, "How can you advocate saving the whales while you deal in dead whale parts?" The answer is simple and reasonable: Selling scrimshaw no longer endangers whales because it is now illegal to import whale teeth into the United States and next to impossible to smuggle them in, and the whales can no longer be killed within American waters under Federal law. Once the existing supply of whale teeth is exhausted, that's it. Scrimshaw collecting will become a matter of reselling or trading in existing pieces. But refraining from selling scrimshaw will not bring back to life the whales whose teeth are now on the market. And Sutherland's store, meanwhile, helps to renew the respect due to an important folk art form that nearly died out a century ago.

A less fortunate result of the revival of interest is that the whale is too often used as an advertising symbol in the Lahaina area, a come-on capitalizing on the old "whaling capital of the Pacific" image.

Somewhat independently of all this commercialism, however, the word spread that the humpbacks come to Maui for Christmas, make love, have babies, and then head back to the Arctic in May. The water area is relatively small, and whale sightings are easy so interest grew naturally. The public interest that developed in the humpbacks was both scientific and commercial. As is true of other whales, the humpback has not been adequately photographed; suddenly, therefore, everyone, including scientific and popular publications, wanted pictures. The *National Geographic Magazine* sent two photographers to Lahaina. They stayed for more than two months, going out almost daily in a small rubber raft seeking pods of humpbacks among which they could swim and photograph. Californian Jill Fairchild and English sculptor John Perry came over to take movies of the whales, but after they were accused of harassing the whales (by Hudnall) in their pursuit of motion pictures, they ended their partnership in their firm, Sea Library; Fairchild returned to California and Perry decided to learn how to run a movie camera himself. The whalewatchers themselves participated in the whale blitzes already described. A writer for the *National Geographic* spent a few days here before going on to join the whalers of New Zealand. A marine biologist for the National Marine Fisheries Service on the Mainland obtained a grant and chartered a boat for a couple of weeks of whalewatching.

Only once did I personally witness what would have constituted harassment, and I was able to put a stop to it. *Vida Mia* and *Rendezvous* both converged on the same pod of whales, the Magnificent Seven, as a matter of fact. A sightseeing helicopter passing over noticed what we were up to, and suddenly three vehicles were zeroing in on the whales. I pointed the situation out to *Rendezvous* skipper Pat Hughes and he immediately changed course, explaining to the passengers that he saw what appeared to be a better situation only a couple miles away. We were in luck; we did find more whales!

Some observers in California claim that the mushrooming business in whalewatching charter cruises has reached the proportions of harassment. This charge was aired widely in national publications in 1976. Unlike the American Cetcean Society's supervised excursions to show schoolchildren the gray whales off California, the purely commercial operators got into the act for pure profit. The didn't have the Society's experience and they didn't necessarily respect the animals they were seeking. Their one and only motive was to sell tickets to their cruises. A tremendous buildup in the boat traffic resulted among the migrating grays.

The man whose complaints were heard the loudest in this respect was Dr. Raymond Gilmore, a member of the American Cetacean Society and an acknowledged expert on the gray whale. He was quoted in the Society's newsletter, *The Whalewatcher*, issue of February, 1976, as saying the following:

> Some private boats whose owners do not know the art of following whales, or who do not care, will rush the whales, revving the motor up and down as they get close. Or they will cross in front of other boats, which are following the whales at a proper slow speed without motor change, and do so whether they wish to see whales or not.
>
> Or they will pass close to a whalewatching boat or between two such boats, directly over the whales, even knowing there are whales in front, when these small boats just wish to get to another place. And there is sometimes aggressive jockeying for a position as close to the whales as possible.
>
> All this harasses the whales and annoys them, and louses up the show. This is overt harassment of the whales, and as such is in direct violation of the federal law as written in the Marine Mammal Protection Act of 1972, and even, I think, in the Whaling Treaty Act of 1936. . . .

Dr. Gilmore briefly discusses the law, which I shall treat in the next chapter. This leads him to comment that the grays will sometimes approach the whalewatchers—just as we have seen the humpbacks do off Maui. Dr. Gilmore continues:

> Sometimes whales will dodge or zigzag, and subsequently surface alongside or directly in front of a boat which has been following cautiously and properly, a little behind and to one side of the

whales. Such near collisions do not constitute harassment. And, although the whales are alarmed by such a close approach, and will dodge again, often to a great distance, they can easily avoid a collision with a slow-moving boat, and will soon settle down again to a slow speed and a regular rhythm of diving and breathing.

Moreover, gray whales will sometimes approach a slow, steadily-moving boat within a few yards—intentionally so—as if from curiosity at the long, whale-shaped hull floating along nearby. They will even run alongside of the boat for some distance, as much as two miles in a half-hour, always near the surface, obviously unafraid and undisturbed—boat-watching, as it were.

Thus, harassment should consist of the activities described above which frighten and annoy the whales, and not consist in a certain, arbitrary minimum-distance between them and the boat.

This last comment is a direct reference to guidelines set down in 1975 by the National Marine Fisheries Service, which comes under the Department of Commerce, and which is the agency that monitors compliance with portions of the Marine Mammal Protection Act of 1972. Their guidelines to whalewatching were contained in a press release issued and reissued during the past two years:

In the case of boats near humpback whales, the NMFS recommends whale watchers observe the following precautions:

1. Do not speed alongside, over, or around whales.
2. Do not speed between whales or through a group of whales.
3. Avoid close encounters. It is recommended that boats stay at least 50 yards away from any whales.
4. Regulate the speed of the boat according to the speed of the whales.

Humpback whales are large, with adults averaging 40 feet in length. Should a vessel collide with a humpback, either accidentally or deliberately, there is a good chance of injuring the whale or damaging the vessel, especially small boats. Injury to any humpback whale is serious, because of the small size of the North Pacific population. In 1972, a Japanese scientist estimated the population at only 1,200.

This particular press release was issued by NMFS Honolulu representative Robert Iversen, and is meant to apply to humpback whalewatching. Similar guidelines were laid down for whalewatching the grays off the Mainland Pacific coast. These suggestions are reasonable and designed both to protect the whales and to aid the whalewatcher in complying with the Marine Mammal Protection Act. Obviously, enforcers realize that whales approach boats, and therefore the fifty-yard limit is designed as an educated recommendation to boat operators. The fifty-yard figure is not written into the law, so neither navigator nor whale will be hauled off to federal court if a whale decides to move in close for some peoplewatching!

Most observers expect that either the law will be strengthened or its present definitions broadened so that within the next two or three years whalewatching will be supervised more strictly. Special permits may be required for boat operators wishing to conduct whalewatching cruises. The flap caused by concerned cetologists in California during the 1976 season was probably justified, and if the law is to be enforced in keeping with its spirit, the controls will come.

Protection and Enforcement

T wo federal laws currently protect cetaceans, as well as a number of other endangered species, in American waters. These laws are the Marine Mammal Protection Act of 1972 and the Endangered Species Act of 1973. It is now appropriate to look at these laws and quote both from them and from the official interpretations of them as contained in the *Federal Register* (Vol. 39, No. 10, January 15, 1974). Misunderstanding, misinterpretation, and misinformation are rampant concerning these laws, especially among those who have not read them.

The first point to clear up—a point that directly affects whalewatching —is the federal government's use of the word *take*, and the effect of that word on the official meaning of the word *harass*. *Take* occurs in the Marine Mammal Protection Act, "Purpose of Regulations" as stated in the Act's introduction and interpreted in the *Federal Register*: "The regulations in this part implement the Marine Mammal Protection Act of 1972 . . . which, among other things, restricts the taking, possession, transportation, selling, offering for sale and importing of marine mammals." Notice that "taking" of marine mammals is thus prohibited by federal law.

Again, to quote from the *Federal Register*: " 'Take' means to harass, hunt, capture, collect, or kill, or attempt to harass, hunt, capture, collect, or kill, any marine mammal . . . or the negligent or intentional operation of an aircraft or vessel, or the doing of any other negligent or intentional acts which result in the disturbing or molesting of a marine mammal." Thus, the harassment of whales is specifically prohibited by the federal government.

A "marine mammal" is defined in these laws as "those specimens of the following orders, which are morphologically adapted to the marine environment, whether alive or dead, and any part thereof, including but not limited to, any raw, dressed or dyed fur or fin: Cetacea (whales and porpoises), pinnipedia, other than walrus (seals and sea lions)."

It is important to understand that these two federal laws, while created a year apart, were meant to act together, hand in glove. Each one strengthens or clarifies the other. For instance, in the Endangered Species Act, dolphins and porpoises are not mentioned specifically as endangered species, but the Marine Mammal Protection Act as just quoted specifically includes all cetaceans, the suborder to which all dolphins and porpoises belong.

Not all species of whales are considered endangered. The Endangered Species Act lists eight: blue, bowhead, finback, gray, humpback, right, sei, and sperm. The wording of the Marine Mammal Act, however, makes it obvious that all whales are protected. This is why American tuna fishermen are federal criminals in the whalewatchers' book. They follow the porpoises because they know that porpoises travel with the tuna. They drop nets which then entangle the little whales along with the tuna, and because the porpoise breathes air, it drowns when forced to remain under water for the length of time it takes the fishermen to complete their catch. Also on record are numerous accounts of American tuna fishermen mercilessly clubbing porpoises and dolphins to death in the nets, rather than assisting them to escape, as the law requires.

In May, 1976, conservationists sued to force the tuna industry to comply with the law which protects the dolphins. Experiments with new nets, including those with the "Medina trapdoor," which allows some of the netted dolphins to escape and still leaves the tuna inside, had not been as successful as hoped. On May 12, U.S. District Judge Charles R. Richey, sitting in Washington, D.C., ruled that the present methods of netting tuna violate the law. He quoted sources saying that these methods result in the death of 350,000 dolphins a year. (This is a reduction from the amount killed before the introduction of the Medina net and other fishing methods. And at the end of 1976, it was found the kill rate had been reduced to 100,000 for the year. Conservationists, however, still consider this number unacceptable.) In his decision, Judge Richey wrote, "The interests of the marine mammals come first under the statutory scheme, and the interests of the [tuna] industry, important as they are, must be served only after protection of the animals is assured."

In answer to the tuna industry's cries that hunting for tuna on their own without the aid of the accompanying porpoises is too costly, the judge wrote, "But steps which ensure the protection and conservation of our natural environment must, almost inevitably, impose temporary hardships on those commercial interests which have long benefitted by exploiting that environment." As always, whether the realm be mining, lumber, or tuna fishing, the modern struggle is between money and nature.

The tuna industry immediately recruited the support of California Congressman Robert Leggett, who used his office to find a way to circumvent the law. He decided that the best way to do this was to introduce legislation exempting dolphins and porpoises from the Marine Mammal Protection Act. This strategy, in human terms, is reminiscent of the old parody on America's founding principle, "All men are created equal—but some are a little more equal than others."

Here in Hawaii this particular tempest has no local impact. Hawaii tuna fishermen work with hooks and lines, not nets. California fishermen apparently tried their netting methods in Hawaiian waters, but because of the currents and other aspects peculiar to the Islands' waters, the nets were inefficient. The pole and line method was used widely by California fishermen until about 1960, when they discovered that the purse-seine net was less work. The porpoises could escape if they stayed on top and swam over the net; but if they dived, they would be trapped as the net was "pursed" at the bottom, and they would drown. Now most, but not all of the American catch is made by the purse-seine method.

The tuna people are weeping all the way to the bank. Statistics for 1974, for example, indicate that more than 657 million pounds of tuna were bought in the United States at a cost of $1 billion. The figures break down to nine pounds per household at a yearly cost of $14. Judge Richey used figures furnished by the government. They stated that from 1970 to 1972, about 600,000 porpoises died in purse seines.

The two animal-protection laws have other imperfections, too, but some were dictated by what the lawmakers considered to be Constitutional guarantees. For example, Indians and Eskimos are exempted from upholding the provisions of the laws if they live in "native" villages, just as the Columbia River Indians may fish in their traditional—albeit wasteful—methods, a fact which causes hard feelings among the non-native salmon fishermen there. Therefore, native Alaskans are allowed to take whales, walruses, and the like by native methods "if such taking is

primarily for subsistence purposes. . . ," and they may use the "parts"
—that is, ivory, for the making of "traditional native handicrafts." This
exemption has given the Eskimos a large loophole to walk through; they
are now the only Americans who can produce scrimshaw on ivory taken
since the law went into effect. The unfortunate result, I am told by a
number of people who have come to Hawaii from Alaska, is that you
now see quantities of walrus slaughtered, their ivory removed and their
meat left to rot.

The Acts also allow the taking of live marine mammals by special
permit for scientific reasons or educational displays. This provision led to
a confrontation of sorts during the month of March, 1976, in Washington's Puget Sound. The great increase in whale awareness manifested
itself yet again, and this time the outcome was a happy one.

Sea World, Inc., of San Diego, California, had an old permit allowing
it to capture four orcas for training and display. But Sea World's timing
was bad in 1976. They chose to take the orcas at the same time that The
First International Orca Symposium was being held at Evergreen State
College at Olympia, within sight of where the whale trapping took
place!

The American Cetacean Society's *Whalewatcher* for March, 1976, described what happened:

> Just before the capture took place, a large male shepherded a
> small calf out of the nets, and they disappeared. Later, a third one
> got away, in spite of the fact that planes dumped explosives in the
> water to frighten the whales into the nets. But this particular one
> maintained a vigil outside the nets enveloping the other five for
> almost a week.
>
> Interestingly enough, scientists with sophisticated electronic
> equipment were unable, during the first couple of days, to hear any
> kind of communication among the whales, although their breathing
> made plenty of noise, and could be heard for a great distance across
> the water.
>
> In the days that followed, the waters were filled with boats, and
> the air above filled with airplanes. (In fact, one such plane dropped
> flowers on the boats and the whales. This resulted in a sudden order
> that went out Saturday night, that no plane was to fly lower than

3,000 feet above the whale pens, nor within a radius of three miles.) The boats were a little harder to handle. Indeed, one large lumber boat finally said, in essence, "sorry about all this, but you are holding me up, you and your whales in the middle of the channel. I am going through anyway."

Fortunately for the whales, there was room enough for both at that particular section.

The five animals . . . kept in a double net system, became the target of legal suit and countersuit—which meant almost hourly bulletins to the symposium attendees, bulletins which engendered vast sighs of sorrow, on the one hand, or tremendous cheers on the other, depending on whether a certain judge had said, "Let the animals go," or another had said, "You may keep them, but they must be kept in suitable holding tanks," or, "Some animals have just escaped."

It was, apparently, at the time of the attempt to follow the above order, that two more of the animals escaped. And according to watchers on nearby boats, their reunion with the silent circling one (outside the whale pens) was a pageant of beauty and movement. "Like birds they flew" around the boats, under them, between them, in unison, "so great was their joy at being reunited." After some 20 minutes of this, the three took off up the Sound, leaping together in great swoops until they disappeared.

That left three—and one of them was too long, under the permit, so has already been given to Dr. Erikson of the University of Washington as one of 10 animals he has been given permission to have to bolt a type of "fender" onto the dorsal fin with a radio transmitter attached. The "fender" is, it is said, to be bolted on with steel bolts (not magnesium type, which would react electrolytically in sea water to corrode and fall off) although the useful life of the transmitter pack is very short. The question that arises, according to the experts, is just how much will this "fender" affect the hydrodynamics of the cutting edge of the whale's dorsal fin as it knifes through the water? Is this harassment?

It has also been pointed out that much of the same kind of material Dr. Erikson hopes to gain is already available in the work of Dr. Michael Bigg who has, with visual sightings, managed to come up with the involved family relationships of four resident pods of orcas over a three-year period. (This particular pod was a transient one.)

In the meantime, the Washington Senate Commerce Committee approved a bill banning the capture of killer whales for display in commercial attractions, a move which may make history by trying to override the provisions of the Federal Marine Mammal Protection Act. Pressure is also on the governor to declare Puget Sound at least a wildlife refuge, if not a sanctuary. And on the other Washington front—D.C., that is, the House passed legislation authorizing $30.5 million for programs to protect and preserve endangered species of both animals and plants.

Since that *Whalewatcher* story was published, the large orca was released and the remaining two which had not escaped or been set free were fitted with the radio transmitters and released. Dr. Al Erikson has said that the two orcas with transmitters will be used to study "migration and other behavior patterns," and that the mechanisms will eventually fall off the whales.

Further, Puget Sound was declared a sanctuary, and Sea World has agreed to exercise its rights under the permit and attempt to trap the five orcas to which it is entitled outside that area.

The idea of whale sanctuaries appears to be catching on. Sanctuaries are a natural outgrowth of protections already in existence. Game and bird sanctuaries on federal, state or county levels have been known since the last century. This century has seen the introduction of underwater reserves and preserves. That the whales should have their own protected areas seems quite natural. Those who propose them do not feel the idea clashes with the federal laws, but rather affirms them.

Marine mammals have been getting more official recognition and protection from the states in recent years. The State of Florida adopted the manatee as its state marine mammal. Connecticut adopted the sperm whale. The gray whale was adopted as California's marine mammal as of January, 1976, somewhat by default. The decision took effect because the State Legislature agreed on it even though the inscrutable Governor Jerry Brown declined either to sign it or veto it.

Early in 1976 the Maui Chapter of the American Cetacean Society, working through its state representative, Ronald Y. Kondo, proposed that the humpback whale be named the state's official marine mammal. Representative Kondo told me that when he went around to get signatures on his resolution, "I never got so many horse laughs in my life," but every last state representative did sign it. Lahaina's Chuck Sutherland, as president of Maui's American Cetacean Society Chapter, then went to Honolulu to testify in favor of the proposal. Waikiki aquarium director Leighton Taylor, a city employee, and a State Department of Land and Natural Resources representative testified that the monk seal would be a better example, but both lost out. Sutherland said Taylor apparently had some qualms about testifying against the humpback because, he told Sutherland, as he was sitting in his aquarium office preparing his testimony, he looked out his window and saw three humpbacks cavorting off Waikiki—a very unusual place to sight them. He said he wondered if the whales weren't trying to tell him something!

In his testimony Sutherland pointed out that the humpback has been coming to Hawaii since long before human visitors have, and that the humpback is born in Hawaii and is therefore a native citizen. Taylor's argument was that the monk seal is found only in Hawaii, is endemic—that is, is born here—and doesn't leave. Sympathetic legislators, however, seized on Sutherland's statement that the humpback is also born here, and furthermore is seen by vast numbers of people. Only the select few who can make the special trip to the seal's hideaway habitat ever see that animal first-hand. Another state senator, Jean King, jokingly remarked that since the humpback is transient like a tourist, it should, perhaps, be subject to a tourist tax. Finally, no one could come up with a good reason to vote against the Kondo resolution. It passed in both houses, and the humpback is now Hawaii's official marine mammal. Dr. Taylor was a good sport about the outcome, Sutherland told me, and said that he may propose that the monk seal be adopted as the state's official *maritime* mammal at the next legislative session! Meanwhile, Hawaii's Governor George R. Ariyoshi signed the humpback proclamation on June 9, 1976.

Meanwhile, Maui's whalewatchers have inspired a movement that may eventually result in the establishment of another whale sanctuary— this one in some ways even more far-reaching than the one at Puget Sound. This project would bring into play another level of government:

the county. If concern for cetaceans were officially expressed at the federal, state, and county levels, it would appear that public awareness has been thoroughly aroused.

The proposal for Maui County is that the heart of the humpback country be designated the Maui County Whale Preserve; and the language of the proposed resolution specifically uses the word *sanctuary*. Maui County consists of four islands: Maui, Molokai, Lanai, and Kahoolawe. The "humpback nursery" of Maalaea Bay is located at a point where West Maui (the location of Lahaina) narrows down to the isthmus known as Central Maui. Central Maui is the base of the tremendous (10,020 feet) dormant volcano Haleakala, which forms the rest of Maui. The far end of Maalaea Bay and the waters associated with it end at the south at La Perouse Bay. Directly across is the eastern tip of Kahoolawe. To the north is Lanai, and opposite it on West Maui, Lahaina. At the far north is the tip of (West) Maui, and some twelve miles across the channel is the eastern tip of Molokai. All the water within these boundaries is designated as the proposed county whale preserve because this is where the humpback activity is heaviest.

If the proposal becomes a reality, the preserve would become a sort of county park and would require some county rangers—"whale rangers," if you will. Maui County parks at present only employ personnel in what would be described as maintenance jobs. Rangers or wardens such as some Mainland county parks have would be required. Hopefully, they would have a small (18 to 21 foot) power boat with which to track down people observed harassing the whales. The overall result of establishing the sanctuary, however, would be the same as that of naming the humpback the official state marine mammal: It would bring attention to the public concern for the future of cetaceans.

Present at one of the early meetings in Lahaina where the proposal was to be outlined was Project Jonah's Joan McIntyre. She wisely cautioned that this proposal, like any similar activity elsewhere, should not appear to have originated from the outside, but rather that the government officials should feel it was the desire of their own citizens. This is excellent philosophy in such an undertaking and, in this instance proved extremely relevant. Joan just happened to be visiting Hawaii during this meeting, and she attended out of personal interest. Maui citizens initially behind the proposal were Chuck Sutherland; Michael Wyatt, a Lahaina sculptor who is also a member of the Maui Chapter of the American Cetacean Society; Jim Luckey, general manager of the Lahaina Restoration Foundation which maintains, among other projects, the "World of the Whale" exhibit aboard its ship, the *Carthaginian II*; Rick Gaffney, Maui representative of the University of Hawaii's Sea Grant program; and myself.

The Puget Sound idea will doubtless have other offshoots (if the Maui idea can, in fact, be classified as such). The sanctuary or preserve designation has a number of ramifications, not all of them clear at this writing. For instance, some members of the Maui whalewatchers believe that the hydrofoils operated by the SeaFlite Corporation are a menace to the humpbacks and constitute harassment according to the definition of the Marine Mammal Protection Act. To clarify, a hydrofoil is a large, boat-like passenger vehicle which was introduced to Hawaiian waters in 1975 as a means of interisland transportation. Beneath the hull of the hydrofoil are suspended "foils," which look and act like airplane wings. The foils, however, are smaller than wings because they go through water, which is denser than air. When extended, the foils reach down twelve feet. Once the hydrofoil has attained its speed, it lifts its hull off the water, thus reducing the drag and making the fast ride possible. On its hull, a hydrofoil can go 15 to 16 knots. Up on its foils it cruises at 41 knots. The jet airplane's engine gets its thrust by taking in air, compressing it in the engine, and expelling it out the back. The hydrofoil engine gets its power by sucking in water and shooting it out the back at the rate of 45,000 gallons per minute.

What effect would the establishment of a County Whale Preserve have on SeaFlite? Could it halt their operation in Maui waters? Probably not, because a good attorney could argue that the hydrofoils were there before the law was passed, and elsewhere, in other matters, putting someone out of business after they have been legally established has been ruled unconstitutional.

Whether one wishes to give credit or to blame someone for arousing public concern over the hydrofoil versus whale issue, that "someone" has to be me. I first raised the question of possible harassment in my capacity as a reporter for *The Maui News*, and followed through with an article in *Honolulu Magazine*, November, 1975. The Maui Chapter of the American Cetacean Society became the official torchbearer of the cause against the hydrofoils, and it is to Chapter President Chuck Sutherland's credit that the issue was never allowed to become an emotional one—in Chuck's shoes I probably would not have been able to exert the same control. But once I had written the articles and raised the issue, I decided that as a reporter I should sit back, let the issue take its natural course, and report on it rather than fan the flames.

I found that a number of people were willing to carry on the idea. Sea Grant's Rick Gaffney and Sea Life Park's Ed Shallenberger both stated that the essence of the danger derived from the fact that the hydrofoil is something foreign to the sea. It is so much faster than anything the cetaceans have ever encountered before, even though they can surely hear the hydrofoil underwater, that they have no way of estimating how much time they have—or do not have—to get out of the way.

To back up my contention that a hydrofoil-whale collision is a real possibility I wrote a story based on the findings of a Navy board of inquiry which was set up to investigate the collision of a Navy hydrofoil and a gray whale in January, 1975, in San Diego Bay. The gray died. SeaFlite officials tell me that the accident was fatal because the Navy hydrofoil had a screw (propellor), and the SeaFlite hydrofoil does not. I never quite understood the connection, because I could not accept the argument, if that is what they intended, that their hydrofoil would therefore not cause fatal injuries. Boeing, manufacturers of SeaFlite hydrofoils, claims that a foil will withstand a crash with a log eighteen inches in diameter. A vehicle with such a guarantee hitting a humpback's living flesh would cut and no doubt kill. It would also undoubtedly shake up the hydrofoil passengers as well, though how seriously, we don't know. Fortunately, SeaFlite passed the 1976 whale season without colliding with a whale. A small number of dolphins were reportedly killed, however, and a larger number of fish.

To SeaFlite's credit, they eventually reacted positively to public concern. First, they changed their course during the height of the humpback season; instead of going through the heart of the whale waters, between Lahaina and Lanai, they went between Kahoolawe and Lanai. Whales frequent those waters, too, but apparently they are not so densely concentrated there. Also, the sight of the hydrofoil was more distant, and therefore less abrasive to Maui whalewatchers. Second, they made $3,000 cash plus air and hydrofoil transportation available to Shallenberger and his authorized assistants to conduct the Whale Blitz—the

A SeaFlite hydrofoil.

humpback census. SeaFlite announced that they wished to learn through the census where the main whale concentrations tended to be so that they could avoid such a course. One big concern was Maalaea Bay—the humpbacks' nursery—since SeaFlite terminal is located there. SeaFlite said its captains had been instructed to come down off the foils upon approaching the bay and to go through the bay to the terminal at hull speed. It appears that the skippers often did this, but not always.

The concern generated on Maui caused famed Hawaii photographer and conservationist Robert Wenkam, Pacific representative of The Friends of the Earth, to put out a press release. In it he indicated that the organization would take action under federal law if a collision did take place. They needed a collision, however, to make a legal point.

His press release, dated October 31, 1975, read, in part:

> Early reports from SeaFlite corporation, operators of the Boeing jet-foils, indicated complete unconcern for the whales, their spokesman saying, "The whale would be sliced up by the underwater foils. There would be no harm to the passengers." The stainless steel foils extend 12 feet below the hull and are normally six feet beneath the water surface.
>
> In recent months jet-foil captains have become beligerent in their replies to oral inquiries by traveling environmentalists aboard their vessels, accusing them of unwarranted criticism of the company and their operations. . . . In addition to possible death for the whales, some cetacean watchers contend that the jet-foils will seriously interfere with the whales' breeding habits because of the boats' unusual highpitched underwater noise. . . .
>
> Friends of the Earth has conferred with local officers of ACS (American Cetacean Society) and informed SeaFlite that FOE's Washington, D.C. office is prepared to take immediate action to implement provisions of the Endangered Species Act permitting citizens' arrest and legal injunction procedures to stop SeaFlite operations if the firm "harasses, takes or kills" endangered whale species protected under federal law.
>
> Another concern expressed by local divers and fishermen is the possible adverse consequences of blood and fish remains in the water whenever a whale or porpoise strike occurs due to jet-foil operations, thereby increasing the shark hazard.

The one really positive step that Maui whalewatchers took on this issue during 1976 demonstrated the extent of the general public's concern over the plight of the whales. A group of observers was formed; there were always enough of them to man a point near the entrance to Maalaea Bay twice a day to watch the two arrivals and departures of SeaFlite. They chose a point where they could see much of the bay and, on the other side of the spit of land, the open sea through which the hydrofoils came. Sea Grant obtained citizen band radios, and the observers, with SeaFlite's permission, warned the hydrofoil skippers if there were whales in the vicinity. This location was considered crucial because it is, as mentioned, the heart of the humpback nursery. It is also where the channel narrows, and where the SeaFlite terminal is located. The observers report that the hydrofoil captains always acknowledge contact, although with varying degrees of enthusiasm.

Awareness that the cetaceans of the world are being killed off at a rate which will lead to certain extinction, and concern that this should not happen, have given birth to a number of organizations around the world dedicated to saving whales and dolphins. Some are small and with a single purpose, such as the Mendocino Whale War, a neighborly group in the town of Mendocino on the coast of Northern California. They sponsor a woman who broadcasts, in Russian, to Russian whalers at sea. It is hoped that she can touch the conscience of these men and convince them to defect to the United States rather than to continue their whaling. She broadcast during the 1975-76 winter and promised the Russians food, a place to live, and help in learning an American trade. This same town also launched a boycott of Russian and Japanese goods that was felt in its own small way: Sake and Japanese beer have been taken off store shelves in Mendocino, and one restaurant stopped serving Japanese noodles. An advertising man in Hawaii turned down two Datsun accounts.

The Sierra Club, Friends of the Earth, and the Audubon Society all sponsor whale conservation projects. The American Cetacean Society has grown to be the largest of the single-purpose groups, and it has received a long list of requests to open chapters. As of this writing, the society is composed of the mother society in Los Angeles and chapters in San Diego and Maui. The society expects to grant requests ranging from

Canada to Fiji. Another California organization, Project Jonah, is well-known, especially through its leader, Joan McIntyre and the book she edited called *Mind in the Waters*.

Greenpeace operates out of Vancouver, British Columbia, with a branch in San Francisco, and this group believes in the direct approach. They are credited with convincing the government to ban the taking of live orcas off that coast and it is believed the Puget Sound sanctuary will become official because of this example.

Greenpeace sponsored a yacht in 1975 which went to sea looking for whalers. Organization President Robert Hunter documented the encounter in his 1976 annual report:

> It was not until the 60th day at sea, and a week of picking up radio signals, that we caught our first glimpse of a dragger from the Russian fishing fleet. Two days later, June 27, (1975), we closed in on the whalers from the fleet. . . . But by 10 a.m. there could be no doubt about it any more. We could see the huge factory ship, *Vostok*. . . . Within only a few miles of the nearest harpoon boat, we came across a small dead sperm whale. . . . "My God, it's just a baby!" cried Carlie Trueman, 26, the only woman on board. . . . Within minutes, we had four people circling the dead whale in a rubber boat with our crewman [Paul] Watson clambering on top of it for an accurate length measurement later. . . . The whale measured 25 feet, which is under legal minimum size of 30 feet (imposed by the International Whaling Commision). . . .

The Greenpeace people took the most direct of approaches. When they spotted a pod of sperm whales, they sent a rubber boat to go between the whales and the Russian harpoon boat:

> As they [the whales] blew, rainbows formed in the spray. The sight was so beautiful—and so horrifying with the great iron killer boat coming chasing down behind us—that for the first time, tears leapt to my eyes and I was partially blinded for a moment. That was when I heard the sound of the harpoon going off, and the sword-like whish of the cable whipping out behind it, slashing the water less than five feet from the port side of our rubber boat. . . . Thor-

oughly shaken, we pulled the rubber boats back up onto our deck.
. . . There were still eight live sperm whales fleeing toward the
horizon. . . . As far as we could tell, the eight surviving whales
managed to get away—for one more day, at least. . . .

In 1976 Greenpeace leased another boat for still another mission to
harass the whale-hunters. The boat was a converted American minesweeper leased out of Seattle by the Canadian environmentalists. They
came to Lahaina early in August, 1976, and I was able to interview both
Hunter and Dr. Paul Spong, the New Zealand-born psychologist mentioned elsewhere in this book.

They had encountered a Japanese whaling fleet within six hundred
miles of Hawaii, Hunter told me, but they later lost track of them. "Looks
like the fleet pulled out right away (after being sighted by Greenpeace),"
he said. "It seems to be the pattern. They have good public relations. The
last thing the Japanese want is exposure."

In mid-July, he said, they'd also encountered a Russian whaler—this
one within eight hundred miles of Hawaii. Hunter said that the Russians
had a dead sperm whale in tow, and Greenpeace spent forty hours
harassing the whalers. There was no confrontation, however, and the
Greenpeace people went to Honolulu for supplies. There they were
given food, and the *James Bay*, their minesweeper, was completely fueled
by sympathizers. They then came to Lahaina for a few days.

In an interview I conducted with Hunter and Spong, Hunter confirmed that the Japanese and Russians kill 80 percent of the whales killed
worldwide. He agreed that International Whaling Commission controls
are "meaningless," saying, "They claimed to have impartial IWC observers aboard every ship, but we've found they have Japanese observers on Russian ships, and Russian observers on Japanese ships. . . .
Their whole thing about objective control is a lie."

In the same interview, Spong said: "What we are dealing with is the
last of the great whales. They are verging on commercial extinction,
which borders onto biological extinction."

Asked what good it does to "harass" the whaling fleets, Spong said,
"It raises the level of public awareness. . . . It brings about public and
political pressure." To that Hunter added that the whaling companies are
now financially in such a position that "if we can cut in five percent of
their business, they might as well not go out next year."

Greenpeace's leased minesweeper, the James Bay.

Other groups, some much larger than those described, are involved in the anti-whaling work. One such is the Animal Welfare Institute in Washington, D.C. This group has launched, with some success, a drive to boycott Japanese goods until Japan stops whaling. The institute also urges adults and schoolchildren to flood foreign embassies with letters of protest not only to Japanese and Russian embassies, but also to firms which import Japanese products. They report replies from Datsun, among others, which indicate considerable irritation.

The institute keeps members and friends abreast of developments by means of a newsletter. One sent out back in September, 1975, is typical of those before and since in its pessimistic appraisal of the International Whaling Commission. The newsletter recalled that after the 1973 IWC meeting in London, both Japan and Russia stated that they simply would not observe the whale-kill quotas allotted them. The newsletter also expressed the feeling that the IWC meetings served rhetorical purposes only. The commission does bring together people from various parts of the world with information on whale populations, but this pool of information tends to indicate merely that whales are still on the road to oblivion. The newsletter noted that international conservation groups observing the 1975 IWC meeting "voiced discouragement at the Commission's actions and once again called for the 10-year moritorium recommended by the United Nations."

The institute's publication continued:

> At the 1974 meeting the moratorium was cast aside in favor of a management scheme which, in theory, would give protection to the most depleted species and stocks. This year, however, when the implementation scheme came to a vote, the whaling interests again were able to apply enough pressure on the Commission to obtain major compromises.
>
> On key quotas, the Scientific Committee's recommendations were ignored where they did not fit in with industry requirements. . . . By the time the seemingly endless compromises had been haggled out, 32,578 great whales were scheduled for death by the explosive harpoons of IWC nations. The Commission took no action on behalf of the small whales currently being slaughtered despite a thorough report on dangers to their populations submitted by the Interna-

tional Union for the Conservation of Nature. . . . The large majority of the Scientific Committee has or had connections with the whaling industry. Few of its members have any compunctions about whale killing for profit.

That late-1975 newsletter expresses the institute's belief in the effectiveness of a boycott: "The IWC still belongs to the old guard. Yet this year's quota cuts (approximately 8,500 whales) were larger than any ever adopted in the past. The boycott and demonstrations have had an effect. Their continuance is essential if further needed protection for the whales is to be won."

The American Cetacean Society, on the other hand, does not believe in the boycott approach. In explaining the society's position on boycotts in February, 1976, at a meeting of the Maui Chapter, Bemi De Bus, one of the ACS founders, said, "We feel this is a lopsided approach to the situation. . . ," adding that there were a number of other ways to attack the matter, including, at the national level, the use of the 1967 Fishermen's Protective Act, and the Pelly Amendment to that federal act, passed in 1969. The act itself permits the halting of importation of foreign fish products if they are "not caught in what we consider the right way." The Pelly Amendment allows the President to issue such an order without going through bureaucratic measures. Mrs. De Bus went on: "We say to the Japanese—your whaling is worth $33 million today, and you say you need the whale as a source of protein. You send us $225 million worth of sea food products alone every year. It is high in protein. So, we don't really quite believe it. . . . How about trading off your $33 million for the $225 million? . . . We think this is the way to stop them."

About the Russian whaling industry she had this to say: "Most of the (Russian kill) goes to feed the mink. We'd like to say—maybe you need the mink in Siberia, but we can do without it here. Some people want us to get emotional about saving the whales," Mrs. De Bus concluded. "They want us to endorse a boycott, but the American Cetacean Society is not prepared to do this."

Evaluations as to how effective the boycott approach is vary greatly. Those who support boycotts claim inroads, if not outright success. Various organizations maintain boycotts in countries around the world, but they are spotty; their overall effect is unknown. But in May, 1976, the

Japanese claimed that the ill feeling caused by environmentalists, if not the boycotts themselves, had caused them to force six fishing companies to close down their whaling divisions and establish one joint venture to do all the whaling. The new company is called Nippon Kyodo Hogei Company, and it claims that while some three thousand persons were employed in whaling before, the new company has jobs for less than half that number. The new company reportedly bought three mother ships and twenty catcher ships for whaling. A government spokesman said that some of the leftover catchers will be converted into tugs or patrol boats.

In releasing this information the Japanese claimed that they were forced to reduce their whaling efforts because the International Whaling Commission had finally yielded to international public pressure and lowered the Japanese kill quota. This claim, I firmly believe, is not true. The message is far more ominous. If the Japanese had been hurt by the quota reduction alone, they would have done what they did in previous years: They would have refused to abide by the IWC quota, shamelessly announcing their refusal to the world.

What has really happened, and the IWC's Scientific Committee has hinted at this in past years, is that the numbers of the whales are now so diminished that the Japanese cannot even fill their allotted kill quota. The whaling industry has reached the point where it has overkilled to the verge of putting itself out of business. The Scientific Committee has found that in recent years the Japanese and other whaling nations have not been able to reach their quotas. The committee members have therefore asked these countries why they object to lower quotas. The unspoken answer is that the whaling nations want the higher quotas maintained just in case their fleets get lucky and are able to meet the higher kill-count.

The real message in the "voluntary" fleet reduction by the Japanese is, therefore, very clear: There are no longer enough whales left to make whale hunts on the scale they were formerly conducted profitable.

Even the whalermen of the past century were impressed with the obvious intelligence of the cetaceans. Those who wrote stories, or told them to others for the writing, never failed to marvel at one act or another which indicated intelligence rather than instinct, which determines most of the behavior of the majority of the animals. I like to think that the ancient whales acted out of conscious decision rather than instinct when they returned to the sea, that they rationally chose to avoid the increasing competition on land for food. Many other animals remained on land and became extinct. Perhaps the human race should rejoice in the whale-ancestors' decision—if decision it was—to return to the sea. For who can tell? Had it stayed on land, the whale, with its paralimbic lobe, may have become the earth's dominant animal. In retrospect it is difficult to image the ego of *Homo sapiens* tolerating such a development!

It is therefore ironic that a warfare for superiority which failed to take place on land has, in a sense, taken to the water. In the old days, before the Foyn harpoon gun was invented, perhaps the hunting of whales was forgivable, since whalers had not yet learned that they were killing fellow intelligent beings. Judging by our record, however, knowledge of the whales' nature probably would not have made any difference, anyway.

The Japanese, who seem to be taking the brunt of the conservationists' ire because the Russians are less accessible, have at least shown twinges of conscience over the matter. The Japanese government has caused to be established what is known as the Japan Whaling Information Center in New York City. However, the U.S. Department of Justice requires American firms acting as agents for foreign governments to so state; and the "information center" press releases show that the center is, in fact, International Public Relations Co., Ltd., of the same address as the center. This center has put out some gems, and one of its recurrent themes is that Japan needs to keep killing whales to supply protein for its people. Yet these killers of the sperm whale do not eat the sperm whale. And, as Mrs. De Bus pointed out above, the food products Japan exports every year would go a long way toward meeting the country's protein needs.

"Reasons" also degenerate into excuses in Japanese pro-whaling propaganda: "In Japan, however, U.S. conservationist demands that the Japanese abandon whale meat consumption seem inconceivable—as farfetched as Japan insisting that Americans abandon hamburger or sirloin steak." (From their press release of November, 1974).

It is, of course, absurd to compare the hamburger and sirloin intake of the Americans to the 6 percent that whale meat adds to the Japanese protein consumption. At one time the Japanese claimed that it was the low cost of whale meat that made it essential to a certain segment of the population. Whale meat prices have risen in Japan way out of proportion to the increase in the cost of other meats, so that argument is no longer valid. The innuendo in this statement by the "information center" is that whale meat is as much a part of the "Japanese way of life" as hamburgers (or hot dogs or apple pie) are to the "American way of life."

No matter how much we study the whale, it seems some misbeliefs continue to survive. Why is the orca still called "killer whale"? This largest of the porpoises will, indeed, kill a whale when hungry. It does so as an organized group activity, not singly and not wantonly. But the misnomer "killer" sticks and, among the uninformed, causes fear. In the winter of 1975-76, various yachting magazines carried articles about the "danger" that yachts could be sunk by whales, usually "killer" whales. These warnings were largely based on separate incidents in 1973 and 1974, in which two sailboats were separately rammed and sunk in the region of the Galapagos Islands, off Ecuador. In the overwhelming majority of brushes between yachts and whales, however, the whales have gone to considerable lengths to avoid collisions.

In an effort to come up with an explanation for these seemingly deliberate rammings, I refer back to my description of "surface traveling." I was impressed, when watching the whales at this activity, that they did not look about, but that they seemed to have only one thing in mind: getting to their destination. They seemed to be so single-minded in doing so that perhaps they were oblivious to anything else. I feel they could easily have hit something in their way, unless they were deliberately thinking about watching out for traffic. Or, taking another approach, Victor Scheffer has written that the sperm whale is exceptionally possessive about territorial rights. It is possible that a sperm whale could ram a boat or anything else that seemed to be menacing his territory. But most of all, those who have attempted to explain the sinkings report that not just one, but several whales—a family pod—were sighted in the area. If any one whale had been inadvertently hit or even thought he had been threatened, and especially if a baby were concerned, a parent or guardian most certainly would attack. But no evidence indicates that the whales wantonly or haphazardly attacked a boat; they acted deliberately, though their reasoning is, so far, beyond us. In one instance—the sinking of Dougal Robertson's *Lycette*—the survivors were in a life raft but were not attacked; they didn't even see whales again, thus ruling out the idea the whales had anything against them. The *Lycette* had apparently been the offender—though how she offended, the passengers never knew—and once the offender had been taken care of, the matter was clearly over with, to the whales' way of thinking.

These unexplained incidents seemed to have generated an unjustified hysteria among some who fear that whales have declared war on peoples' yachts. During the 1975 Trans-Pac (the Trans-Pacific Yacht Race from Los Angeles to Honolulu, a biannual yachting classic), the skipper of a boat sailing along with the fleet, but not a part of the race, claimed that her boat was sunk after it had been struck by a whale. When the rescued crew reached Honolulu, I talked with some of them, one of whom claimed he had seen the whale *after* the boat was struck. That he did make a sighting at all is nearly impossible, for the incident occurred close to midnight on a moonless night. Not that the whale would have lingered to make sure he had done his job well, anyway! Skippers of some Trans-Pac boats, however, did report a number of partially submerged logs in the area. Still, being attacked by a whale makes a romantic-sounding yarn—lots more interesting than colliding with a floating log.

The overwhelming evidence of all cetacean study, ancient and modern, testifies to the intelligence and the friendliness of these animals. The Greek tales of human friendships with the dolphins must have had some basis in fact upon which the more fanciful tales rested. There must also be something to what I and many others have felt in the presence of the great humpbacks. Somehow these animals have made me feel that they were apprehensive of people and their vehicles, but that they nevertheless wanted to be friends. Every year, the whales' apprehension is obvious at the beginning of the whalewatching season; every year, their apprehension seems to give way to tolerance as they become familiar all over again both with our vessels and with ourselves. They develop a trust, which on rare unfortunate occasions is broken by a drunk driver in a high-powered boat. This trust may also be the undoing of the unlucky whale who finally decides to investigate a hydrofoil, the speed of which is for the moment beyond a whale's comprehension.

With respect to the possibility of a hydrofoil accident, I was very much struck by the condescending comment a SeaFlite corporate official gave to a group of local whalewatchers when we personally confronted him with our fears: "If they're as intelligent as you claim," he said "we'll only hit one. Then the rest will know enough to stay out of our way." He just may be right!

But there are those of us who think that even the sacrificial loss of one humpback is too much and is unnecessary. To us, the attitude expressed by his statement seems callous; to him, we probably sound like a bunch of bleeding hearts.

I much preferred the comment I heard from another stranger sometime later. It was during one of my infrequent trips to the Mainland. As I walked through the downtown airline terminal in San Francisco in April of 1976, I saw a sign which urged, "Protect the Whales." It was inside a travel bureau, so I thought it was advertising a lecture or an exhibit. A man—who looked more like a Marlboro man than a bleeding heart—was behind the counter. I asked the significance of the sign.

"We're just asking people to care about the whales," he told me.

"It's not a lecture, or something?" I countered.

"No. Why, are you concerned about the whales?"

"Very much," I said.

"Good. Because when the last whale dies, we will be next."

Lahaina.

Bibliography

Factual and anecdotal background for this book came from a variety of sources besides my own personal observation, attendance at lectures and conversations with the experts. These include newspaper clippings saved over the years, recent magazine articles, and newsletters from various organizations; these have been credited within the text.

Following is a list of the books relied upon most heavily as sources of fact; they are recommended for the students who want to pursue the study of whales in detail.

Budker, Paul. *Whales and Whaling*. Macmillan. New York, 1959

Bullen, Frank T. *The Cruise of the Cachalot*. Smith. Elder. London, 1898.

Lilly, John C. *Lilly on Dolphins*. Anchor Editions (Doubleday). Garden City, New York, 1975.

MacDonald, Gordon A., and Agatin T. Abbott. *Volcanoes in the Sea*, University of Hawaii Press. Honolulu, 1970.

McIntyre, Joan (editor). *Mind in the Waters*. Charles Scribner's Sons. New York, 1974.

Matthews, Leonard H. (editor). *The Whales*. Crown Publishers. New York, 1974.

Mowat, Farley. *A Whale for the Killing*. Atlantic-Little, Brown. Boston, 1972.

Norris, Kenneth S. *The Porpoise Watcher*. W. W. Norton. New York, 1974.

Ommanney, F. D. *Lost Leviathan*. Dodd, Mead. New York, 1971.

Riedman, Sarah R., and Elton T. Gustafson. *Home Is the Sea: For Whales*. Abelard-Schuman. New York, 1971.

Scammon, Captain Charles M. *The Marine Mammals of the Northwestern Coast of North America*. Dover Publications. New York, 1968.

Scheffer, Victor B. *The Year of the Whale*. Charles Scribner's Sons. New York, 1969.

Slijper, Everhard J. *Whales and Dolphins*. The University of Michigan Press. Ann Arbor, 1976.

Index

(Because the humpback whale is referred to throughout the book, this species has been omitted from the index. Physiological and behavioral specifics of the humpback may be found under the general listing, "whale," or under specific references.)